Zavania is ruled by its very own king and queen, who live in the royal castle together with their son the Crown Prince Frederic and their daughter the Princess Lyra. Lyra's used to parties and jewels and all kinds of magical luxuries — everything a girl could wish for! But will her most important wish come true...?

Look out for Maddie's other
adventures in Zavania . . .

Unicorn Wishes

Mermaid Wishes

Princess Wishes

Carol Barton

Illustrated by Charlotte Alder

Scholastic Canada Ltd.

Scholastic Canada Ltd.
604 King Street West, Toronto, Ontario M5V 1E1, Canada

Scholastic Inc.
557 Broadway, New York, NY 10012, USA

Scholastic Australia Pty Limited
PO Box 579, Gosford, NSW 2250, Australia

Scholastic New Zealand Limited
Private Bag 94407, Greenmount, Auckland, New Zealand

Scholastic Children's Books
Euston House, 24 Eversholt Street, London NW1 1DB, UK

First published in the UK by Scholastic Ltd, 2006
This edition published by Scholastic Canada Ltd, 2006

Library and Archives Canada Cataloguing in Publication
Barton, Carol
Princess Wishes / Carol Barton ; illustrated by Charlotte Alder.
ISBN 0-439-93733-7 (pbk.)
I. Alder, Charlotte II. Title.
PR6102.A75P74 2006   823'.914   C2006-903932-1

ISBN-13 978-0-439-93733-7

6 5 4 3 2 1   Printed in Canada   06 07 08 09 10

Contents

1 The Start of the Adventure   1

2 The Wish   18

3 Mutiny!   34

4 Journey into Zenetzia   49

5 Pigeon Post   66

6 The Blue Parrot   86

7 The Return of the Unicorns   107

8 The Mountains of Cloud   122

9 Hamish McTavock   139

10 Sun Mountain   156

11 The Sun Goddess   174

12 Escape from Sun Mountain   191

13 The Prize   206

For Amy, with love.

Chapter One

The Start of the Adventure

"I heard a rumour that Jessica Coatsworth has got three prizes," said Maddie.

"She'll be unbearable," replied Lucy gloomily. "Do you know which ones she's got?"

"Well, she's bound to get the maths prize," said Maddie as she took her books out of her school bag ready for the morning's lessons, "and probably one for

sport. Let's face it, she's won practically every sports event this year."

"And the third?" said Lucy.

"Don't know." Maddie shrugged. "Knowing her, she'll probably get the headmistress's special prize, for 'the most outstanding girl of her year'."

Lucy giggled at Maddie's perfect imitation of the headmistress's voice. "Do you think you'll get anything, Maddie?" she asked, growing serious.

"Shouldn't think so." Maddie shook her head. "How about you?"

"Doubt it . . . although . . ." Lucy hesitated.

"Yes?" prompted Maddie.

"Those mini pizzas I made were rather good, and my chocolate cake, so I was half hoping for the food technology prize . . ."

"Oh Luce . . . that would be wonderful," said Maddie.

"Well, don't hold your breath," Lucy replied. "Jessica Coatsworth will probably

2

walk off with that one as well. Do you remember, she made those profiteroles when everyone else made flapjacks?"

Maddie sighed. "Well, we'll know this afternoon," she replied.

"Is your mum coming?" asked Lucy as the teacher came into the room.

Maddie nodded. "Yes, she comes every year. I think she always hopes I might get a prize, but I never do. Is your mum coming too?"

Lucy nodded. "Yes. Honestly, it's so embarrassing — especially if we don't get anything. I almost wish they wouldn't come."

"When you girls have quite finished gossiping," said Miss Higgs, "maybe we could get on with the lesson."

"Sorry, Miss," said Lucy.

"Right," said Miss Higgs. "For your homework I asked you to learn the first section of 'Goblin Market' by Christina

Rossetti. I want to see how you got on."

There were groans from around the classroom, and cries of "Haven't learnt it yet, Miss."

"Madeleine O'Neill," said Miss Higgs, "have you learnt the passage?"

"Um, yes, Miss Higgs," Maddie replied.

"Then perhaps you would recite it for us."

* * *

"So who's a right little creep then?" sneered Jessica Coatsworth at breaktime when the girls were sitting on the low wall around the school playing fields.

"What do you mean?" demanded Maddie hotly.

"Learning all that poetry word perfect. Who did you think you were trying to impress?"

"I wasn't trying to impress anyone," retorted Maddie. "I just like learning poetry."

4

"Huh!" Jessica Coatsworth wrinkled her nose in disgust as if she found it impossible to believe that any normal person could actually like learning poetry. Turning to her friends she said, "I suppose she thinks if she's good at learning a few lines everyone will forget her carroty hair and that dreadful brace on her teeth."

"Take no notice, Maddie," said Lucy loyally.

Maddie bit her lip. She was well used to Jessica Coatsworth's taunts about the way she looked, but she longed to say that it was her gift for learning lines that was one of the reasons that her friend Sebastian kept asking her to help him with his work. But she remained silent, for the only time she had mentioned Sebastian and the fact that she went to visit him in Zavania, that strange land where he lived, she'd got the distinct impression that the other girls hadn't believed her.

5

"There's the bell," said Lucy. "Come on." Jumping down from the wall she began to follow the other girls into school, leaving Maddie to follow more slowly. Thinking about Sebastian had made her wonder just when he would come for her again. She knew it would only be when someone made a wish — and then only if Sebastian's boss, Zenith the WishMaster, proclaimed it to be an Official Wish — that Sebastian and Zak the raven would come and collect her for a wish-granting assignment.

She had helped with two wishes now, one to return a baby unicorn to its mother and another to retrieve a mermaid's comb that had been stolen.

Sometimes the waiting between wishes seemed so long to Maddie that she would begin to despair that she would ever see her friends again or return to the land of Zavania where they all lived.

* * *

Maddie's house was quite close to the school so she went home for lunch each day. It was a warm day and Maddie found herself dawdling as she approached the house, dragging her feet a little and walking almost at a snail's pace as she found herself wondering again about the school prizes and who would win them. She had just reached the gate when her mother opened the door.

"Oh, there you are, Maddie," she called. "Come on, hurry up. I've put sandwiches and fruit on the kitchen table for you. I've just got to pop up the road to the post office. I'll get changed when I get back and then we'll go off to the prize-giving."

"All right." Maddie watched as her mother hurried away up the road towards the village and it was then, as she turned to go into the house, that she heard it.

"Psst!"

She stopped and looked round but couldn't see anyone. She was about to go

indoors when it came again.

"Psst!"

She stopped again but she still couldn't see anyone.

"Up here!" someone hissed above her.

Stepping back from the front door, Maddie looked up and there on the telephone wires that ran to the house, flanked on one side by a couple of sparrows and on the other by a white dove, was a large black raven.

"Zak!" Maddie cried out in delight and the two sparrows took flight in sudden alarm. Only the dove remained, cooing loudly and sidling up to the handsome black bird.

"Hi there!" said Zak coolly and knowing him as well as she did, Maddie knew he was showing off to impress the dove.

"Has someone made a wish?" asked Maddie breathlessly.

"Sure thing, kiddo," said Zak, speaking

out of the side of his beak. "Looks like we're in business again. Get yourself down to the willows pronto."

"Oh, wonderful," cried Maddie. But as she made to dash into the house she suddenly stopped and clapped a hand over her mouth.

"What's up?" squawked Zak. He had turned his attentions to the dove again but he paused and peered impatiently down at Maddie.

"I can't," she protested.

"What do you mean, you can't?" demanded Zak. "There's no such word as 'can't'."

"What I mean is," said Maddie, "I have to go to the school prize-giving after lunch with my mother."

"Well, that's after lunch," said Zak. "I'm talking about now."

"Yes, I know, but will I be back in time . . . ?"

Zak gave a great sigh and began strutting up and down along the phone wire under the admiring gaze of the dove. "I would have thought by now you would have known that a trip into Zavania takes no time at all. You have to be back to go to the prize-giving? OK, so you'll be back. No problem. Go and get your lunch. Bring it with you and I'll meet you down under the willows." With that he flapped his wings and turned his back on Maddie, finally able to give his undivided attention to his latest conquest.

With a little chuckle Maddie clapped her hands and ran into the house. At last! she thought as she dashed into the kitchen and picked up her sandwiches, crisps and apple. Pausing only long enough to drink the glass of orange juice her mother had left for her, she hurried out of the back door into the garden munching as she went. At last, someone, somewhere had

made a wish and Zak and Sebastian had come to fetch her to help them to grant it!

There was no sign of Zak as Maddie made her way across the lawn and through her dad's vegetable patch to the willows at the bottom of the garden that concealed the stream. And when she parted the branches of the willows and peered through, to her disappointment there was no sign of Sebastian or his boat either.

Maddie tried to see further upstream by leaning forward, but the willows formed a curtain and here, away from the heat of the midday sun, all was cool and dark and green.

"Sebastian," she called softly. "Sebastian, are you there?"

All remained still and silent and then softly, so softly she was almost unaware of it, ripples formed on the stream and a boat slid into view through the leaves.

And quite suddenly he was there again,

standing at the rear of the boat, guiding it into the bank, the pole in his hands, his cloak thrown back over one shoulder revealing his white shirt with its full sleeves and his black breeches. As he caught sight of Maddie waiting for him a slow smile spread across his face, lighting up his dark eyes.

"Hello Maddie," he said simply.

"Sebastian," she replied, finding she had to blink to fight the sudden tears that sprang to her eyes. "It's been such a long time. I was beginning to think you had forgotten me."

"I would never do that," he said and his voice sounded a little husky, not like Sebastian's voice at all. "I would never, ever forget you, Maddie. But you know Zenith only permits me to enter your world when we have a wish to grant."

"Yes, I know," sighed Maddie. "I just wish there wasn't so much time in between, that's all."

"Well I'm here now. Come on, come

aboard." While steadying the boat with one hand Sebastian stretched out his other hand and helped her aboard.

"Where's Zak?" he asked a moment

later as Maddie sat down in the boat amongst the brightly coloured cushions that were always there.

"You may well ask," said Maddie with a laugh.

"What do you mean?" Sebastian frowned. "Don't tell me he's gossiping again — who is it this time? Starlings? Chickens?"

"Neither actually," said Maddie. "This time it happens to be a rather lovely, pure white dove . . ."

"Don't tell me," sighed Sebastian, rolling his eyes. "That's all we need. Especially right now when everything is so fraught in Zavania."

"Oh?" said Maddie quickly. "What's wrong?"

"Just about everything," said Sebastian grimly. "The place is in absolute uproar."

"My goodness," said Maddie. "Whatever has happened? It's not the Princess Lyra, is it?" Maddie knew the princess was notorious for making wishes for the most ridiculous things and demanding that Zenith proclaim them Official Wishes.

"Actually yes, it is her," said Sebastian.

"Oh no," said Maddie. "So what does she want? To keep dolphins for pets? Or maybe to make apples taste of oranges for a change?"

"No, it's nothing like that this time," said Sebastian. He looked serious and Maddie threw him a quick glance. "It's her brother," he went on, "the Crown Prince Frederic."

"What's he done?" asked Maddie curiously. She had never met the prince and had only heard talk about him, mainly from Zak, who she remembered had once dismissed him as a silly fat boy who stuffed himself on sweets.

"He's run away," said Sebastian.

"What?" Maddie stared at him. This was the last thing she had expected. "Surely not."

"Yes, it's true," Sebastian nodded. "Apparently he went off a couple of weeks ago with some new friends and now says he doesn't want to come back."

"Oh dear," said Maddie. "I bet that's caused a bit of trouble at the royal castle."

"You can say that again." Zak had suddenly appeared on the bank of the

stream and hopped on to the boat.

"So you've decided to join us then," said Sebastian sarcastically.

"I must admit I was in two minds," Zak gave a throaty chuckle.

"Nothing to do with a certain little dove I suppose?" said Sebastian, pushing the boat away from the bank once more.

"Might have been," said Zak. "She said I can call on her on the return journey," he added, plumping out his chest feathers as he spoke.

"So what was her name?" asked Sebastian.

"Delores, actually," Zak replied loftily.

"I want to know about the prince," said Maddie impatiently. "Whatever has the king said about him going off?"

"He wasn't very happy," said Zak.

"That's putting it mildly," declared Sebastian. "In actual fact the king is visiting one of his southern provinces and

although he knows that Frederic has gone off with his friends he doesn't yet know that he doesn't intend returning. The poor queen has had hysterics and has taken to her bed."

"But you say it's the Princess Lyra who has made the wish?" said Maddie in bewilderment.

Sebastian nodded. "Yes, that's right."

"So what is the wish?" asked Maddie.

"The Princess Lyra," he said, "has made a wish that her brother will come home."

"But I don't understand," said Maddie, looking from Sebastian to Zak then back to Sebastian again. "I thought you said the prince doesn't want to come home."

"Exactly," said Sebastian. "That's the problem."

Chapter Two

The Wish

"So why does the princess want her brother to come home?" asked Maddie a little later as they drifted downstream into Zavania. "It doesn't sound like her to be so caring."

"You're right," said Zak with a loud snort. "Usually she couldn't care less about anyone. And usually she's not bothered about Frederic at all."

"What's changed?" Maddie looked up at Sebastian.

"I think she really misses him," he said slowly. "You know, she couldn't be bothered with him when he was around but it's a different story now that he's no longer there."

"So have you any idea where he might have gone?" asked Maddie.

"Not really," said Sebastian. "He's been going out at night rather a lot lately but no one seems sure where he goes. I think it must be where he's met these new friends of his."

"What I can't understand," said Maddie, "is why the king didn't seem too worried about all this, after all, Frederic *is* the Crown Prince."

"I think the king has reached the end of his tether with Frederic," said Sebastian. "He's changed, Maddie. Frederic, I mean. You'd hardly recognize him these days."

"A rebel, that's what he's become," muttered Zak.

"What do you mean?" asked Maddie, wide-eyed. This didn't sound like the silly fat boy she'd heard about in the past whose only concern had been where his next supply of sweets was coming from.

"Well, take his hair," said Zak.

"His hair?" said Maddie faintly.

"Yes. He decided he didn't like it brown so he dyed it bright yellow."

"He'd have something to complain about if it was ginger like mine," muttered Maddie.

"And then as if that wasn't enough," Zak went on, "or so the castle pigeons told me, he comes home one night with a stud in his nose! The king threw an absolute fit apparently and there was a fearful row. Soon after that Frederic left home. The king said to leave him, that he'd soon come running home when he ran out of

20

money. Anyway," Zak continued, obviously enjoying himself, "a few days later the king went off to the South."

"So how do they know the prince doesn't intend coming back?" asked Maddie.

"Apparently he wrote to his sister and told her," Sebastian replied.

"Oh dear," said Maddie, sinking down into the cushions again, "it does sound as if they're having a few problems."

"Thirza is convinced Frederic has been going to the Other Place — to your world, Maddie," said Sebastian, "and that is where he has met his new friends, but then Thirza always thinks anything to do with the Other Place will cause trouble. Apart from you, of course, Maddie," he added hastily. "She likes you."

Maddie remained silent. She could well remember the time when Thirza, the WishMaster's tiny housekeeper, had even been very suspicious of her.

As they left the stream behind and joined the faster flowing river, the light grew brighter and stronger and the colours more vivid. The sky above was bluer than any sky Maddie could remember, the grass in the fields greener and the flowers more beautiful and plentiful than any she had ever seen in her world.

They passed through the gorge with its towering sides of sheer rock, home to Harromin the toad. Today, however, there was mercifully no sign of the evil creature and the friends passed through unchallenged.

"Thank goodness for that," said Sebastian with a sigh of relief. "I didn't fancy a battle with Harromin today."

"I'd soon have sorted him out," said Zak with a sniff. "He's scared of me." Then, as if he'd just remembered something, he cocked his head in Maddie's direction. "This prize-giving you

are going to when you get back — will you be winning anything?"

"I shouldn't think so," said Maddie. "There's nothing much I'm really good at."

"You are good at remembering spells," said Zak with a cackle. "Goodness knows where we would have been in the past without you to learn them. And talking of prizes, let's face it, if Sebastian was as good as you at learning lines, then he would have probably earned his Golden Spurs long ago and been a WishMaster himself by now."

Maddie glanced at Sebastian and saw that he had blushed with embarrassment at Zak's words. She felt sorry for him and gave him a quick reassuring smile behind the raven's back.

In a little while they swept into the reed beds that surrounded the gardens of the royal castle and Sebastian brought the boat into the wooden jetty. Zak took the mooring rope in his beak and

dropped the looped end over a post.

Sebastian leapt ashore and helped Maddie from the boat on to the jetty.

"Do we have to go to Zenith for a briefing?" asked Maddie as they made their way through the castle grounds. On other occasions it had been the WishMaster himself who had given them the information about an assignment, but this time seemed rather different to Maddie, since Sebastian and Zak had given her most of the details already.

"We have to get the spells and the ring to perform the magic from Zenith as usual," said Sebastian. "So we need to go straight to the East Tower."

"I got the impression Zenith doesn't want to be too involved in this wish," said Zak craftily.

"Oh?" said Maddie. "Why is that?"

"So that if anything goes wrong and the king, after his return, demands

explanations, Zenith can blame us and still stay in with the king himself, that's why."

"Be quiet, Zak," said Sebastian sternly. "I'm sure it isn't anything like that at all."

"Wanna bet?" said Zak with a sly chuckle.

The castle seemed very quiet. The flags were still flying from the battlements and the royal guards were on duty at the gates, but there was very little activity and few people about as the friends made their way to the East Tower where Sebastian lived with Zenith, Thirza and Zak.

Thirza met them at the top of the first flight of steps. "Come along," she said by way of a greeting. "You are to have refreshments before your instructions."

"Are we late?" asked Sebastian, anxiously casting his eyes towards the WishMaster's turret room.

"No." Thirza shook her head before turning and bustling away to set the long

wooden table that ran the length of the room behind her. "Actually, Zenith isn't here. He's over at the castle."

"Any update on Frederic?" asked Zak, flying to his perch on the dais at the far end of the room.

"Don't think so," said Thirza as she began to set out goblets and plates around the table. "Zenith's in a bit of a predicament really. There's the king unaware that Frederic has no intention of coming home, there's the poor queen who is utterly distraught and making herself ill with worry, and there's the Princess Lyra who, for once, has made a wish that was so important that Zenith couldn't ignore it and had no option but to make it an official one."

"Just what I said," said Zak smugly. "Zenith won't want to fall out with any of them. That's why he's getting you to do this one, old son." He nodded at Sebastian. "Get this one wrong and

Zenith won't want to know."

"We won't get it wrong, will we, Maddie?" said Sebastian, haughtily drawing himself up to his full height and throwing his cloak over one shoulder.

"Of course we won't," agreed Maddie stoutly. "We haven't got any of the others wrong."

"Well, we'll see," said Zak aggravatingly.

Maddie wasn't really hungry since she'd only eaten her lunch a short while ago, but she forced herself to eat some of the fruit and homemade biscuits that Thirza had prepared for them. She knew that the tiny housekeeper would be offended if she didn't.

They had almost finished the meal when they heard a loud noise as the outer door of the East Tower slammed on the floor below.

"That'll be Zenith now," said Thirza, looking round at Sebastian and Maddie,

who both sat up straight while Zak flapped his wings and strutted up and down on his perch.

The WishMaster began to stamp up the stairs and the friends looked at each other in growing apprehension. A few moments later he flung back the door on its hinges and stood there glowering at them all.

Sebastian rose to his feet but Maddie remained seated at the table.

"So you're here then," said Zenith looking from one to another of them. "Good. Come on up to the turret room for your briefing, then you can be on your way. Hurry up, I don't have all day." With that he turned, swirling his cloak behind him, and disappeared up the second flight of stairs in the far corner that led up to his turret room.

"He's in a funny mood," muttered Sebastian under his breath.

"What did I tell you?" said Zak. "He wants to get shot of all this as fast as he can."

"Go along with you," shooed Thirza. "And don't be so disrespectful," she snapped at the raven, "otherwise you could find yourself spending the rest of your life as a worm, hiding from ravens like you!"

With Zak muttering to himself they left

Thirza clearing the table and made their way up the stairs. When they arrived in the turret room it was to find that Zenith had already unlocked the cabinet on the wall and taken out the two scrolls that contained the spells they would need to help them to grant the wish. He had also removed the casket which Maddie knew would contain the ring Sebastian would wear as the conductor of magic. Maddie also knew from previous occasions that the spells could never leave the turret room and had to be memorized before the friends left on the assignment.

"Do you know what this is all about?" Zenith turned suddenly and glared at Maddie.

She swallowed. Usually she hadn't dared to say if either Sebastian or Zak had given her any inkling as to what a wish might be about, because Zenith was the only one supposed to do that. This time,

however, things seemed rather different, with the WishMaster apparently wanting to hurry everything along.

"I know the Crown Prince Frederic has run away," she said in a clear voice.

"Hmmp!" said Zenith, drawing his fearsome eyebrows into a straight, black line. "What else do you know?"

Maddie hesitated. "Not a lot really," she said at last. "Only that the Princess Lyra has made a wish that her brother should come home and that you have declared this to be an Official Wish. I gather the prince doesn't want to come home so it'll be our job to change his mind — is that right?"

"Well, yes. That's the gist of it," said Zenith, clearing his throat. "Won't be that simple, of course."

"They never are," said Maddie. "But we'll work it out, won't we?" She turned to Sebastian.

"Of course we will," Sebastian replied firmly.

"Right," said Zenith. Maddie thought he sounded relieved, as if he'd been expecting trouble from them. Almost as if he'd thought they might not want to go.

Zak had been quiet until that moment but then he cocked his head and said, "Do we have any idea where Frederic might be?"

"The princess had a postcard from him," said Zenith. "But all it said was that he was enjoying himself with his new friends, that he didn't want to come home and that he didn't want anyone trying to find him."

"Not a lot to go on then," said Zak.

"No," said Zenith. "Not really. Anyway, I'll give you the spells and then maybe you could make a start by finding out where Frederic was going at night. The place where he probably met these new friends of his."

32

"I suppose that would be a start," agreed Sebastian.

"Oh," said Zenith as he unrolled the first scroll, "there is just one other thing." Maddie noticed a shifty look had come into his eyes as he was speaking and he appeared to be avoiding direct eye contact with any of them.

"Yes?" said Sebastian, who didn't seem to have noticed anything untoward.

"The Princess Lyra has insisted on accompanying you on this assignment," mumbled the WishMaster.

"Oh great," croaked Zak. "That's all we need!"

Chapter Three

Mutiny!

"That's enough from you." Zenith glared at Zak.

"Well honestly, I ask you," said Zak. "I would have thought the surest way for an assignment to fail would be to have the Princess Lyra along."

"I can't do much about it," said Zenith. "I had already promised she could accompany Sebastian on a mission. At

least there shouldn't be any danger attached to this assignment. It's all perfectly straightforward. You find Frederic and persuade him to come home with you."

"Sounds a bit of a doddle really," said Sebastian.

"Yes," Maddie agreed dubiously as Zenith opened the casket. "Provided the princess behaves herself." Secretly her heart had sunk when she had heard the princess was to go with them. She had only met her a couple of times and that had been on her first visit to Zavania, when the two girls had taken an instant dislike to each other.

"Because of the nature of this mission I have decided that this ring with its gentle topaz shall be your conductor of magic," said Zenith, withdrawing the ring from its bed of black velvet and beckoning Sebastian forward. "You really shouldn't require anything stronger or more potent than this." As he spoke he slipped the ring

on to Sebastian's finger while Maddie and Zak looked on.

"Now the spells." Peering at the three friends from beneath his black eyebrows, the WishMaster flexed his wrists, unrolled the first of the scrolls of parchment, cleared his throat and began to read.

"Zaroosza Zariskin Zarene
Zollaria Zolluria Zadaz
Bring Amber Light Serene
In the Glow of this Topaz."

"I'm really going to try and learn it this time," said Sebastian, but with a touch of desperation in his voice.

"Hmmp!" said Zenith as if he doubted that was even possible. Without further comment he unrolled the second scroll.

"Zimelda of Zimbarwire
Through Orange Molten Fire

Zinggaskium Ze Zingagic
Flare Now and Work Your Magic."

"I'm sure he deliberately makes them complicated," whispered Sebastian, close to despair.

"Don't worry," Maddie whispered back. "They won't take me long to learn."

"The rules are the same," said Zenith. "You need to memorize the spells before you leave this room. When you use them they have to be word-perfect otherwise they will not work. You must use them wisely and you need not think because there is no element of danger with this assignment that I won't be requiring a full account of your actions."

He paused and looked round at them all, his bald head shining in the glow from the single lantern in the turret room. "Now you must learn the spells, then take yourselves off to the castle to

collect the Princess Lyra."

"I can't wait!" muttered Zak.

"If you feel like that about it, you might as well not go," snapped Zenith.

Maddie looked up sharply. The idea of going on an assignment without the raven was unthinkable.

"You can stay here," Zenith went on, "and help Thirza entertain the wizard who is visiting Zavania from the North."

"Is he the one who came before, the one with the pet magpie?" asked Zak.

"Yes, that's him," Zenith nodded.

"In that case I'll go with Sebastian," said Zak.

"So I'm the lesser of two evils, am I?" asked Sebastian.

"It's that magpie," said Zak. "He's a spiteful brute!"

* * *

A little later they left the East Tower. By this time Zenith had shut himself away in

his turret room with his spells and potions and was probably unaware of their leaving.

It was Thirza who came to the steps to wave them off as she usually did. Sebastian kissed her cheek and on a sudden impulse Maddie bent down and did the same.

"Take care of yourselves," said the housekeeper in her high-pitched, bell-like voice.

"We'll be all right," said Sebastian. "This is not a dangerous one, Thirza."

"Maybe not," said Thirza. "But I would urge caution over anything to do with the Princess Lyra. There's been trouble around that young lady since the day she was born."

"I'll second that," sniffed Zak. "Spoilt little madam."

"Well, keep an eye on them, Zak," said Thirza darkly.

"Yeah, OK." Zak sighed and the three

friends took their leave and made their way across the large courtyard to the main castle buildings.

It was the first time that Maddie had been in the royal castle and she was filled with awe as Sebastian approached the guards and gave their names, saying they were on official business for the WishMaster and were expected by the Princess Lyra.

"Anyone would think they don't know who we are," said Zak with a sniff of contempt as the guard went off to consult someone else before admitting them. "I should say they've seen us just about every day of their lives and they still question us! Too full of their own importance if you ask me."

"They're only doing their job," protested Sebastian.

"Huh!" said Zak, unconvinced.

They were eventually admitted by a

footman in gold-trimmed scarlet and blue livery who took them through the main reception halls to a smaller room where he told them to wait.

"It's very grand, isn't it?" whispered Maddie as she gazed round at the ornate gilt mouldings on the walls, the rich tapestries and the sumptuous furniture.

"I suppose so, if you like that sort of thing," said Zak. "Me, I prefer something a bit more simple . . ."

"This is the royal castle," said Sebastian. "You could hardly expect it to be simple . . ."

"What's that girl doing here?" A voice from the doorway made them all swing round to find that the Princess Lyra had come into the room without them hearing and was standing there, hands on hips, glaring at Maddie.

"Your Royal Highness." With a swirl of his cloak Sebastian executed a deep,

perfect bow and even Zak, for all his earlier bravado, managed a deferential nod of his sleek, black head. "We are at your service," Sebastian added.

The princess, however, seemed

unmoved by this show of respect. "I repeat," she said, her blue eyes narrowing, "What is that girl doing here?"

"This is Maddie," Sebastian began firmly, but a note of unease had crept into his voice.

"I know who she is," snapped the princess. "What I asked was why she is here."

Just for the moment Maddie was too shocked by the princess's rudeness to even think clearly, let alone to speak.

"Maddie always accompanies Zak and me on assignments," said Sebastian.

"Well, I am accompanying you this time," said the princess haughtily.

"Yes," Sebastian agreed. "I know that. Zenith told us you would be coming, but Maddie will be coming with us as well."

"This is *my* wish," said the princess, "and if I say I don't want her to come with us, then she won't come."

"Oh boy," muttered Zak under his breath. "What did I tell you? Trouble from the word go."

"What did you say?" The princess swung round on Zak, who hopped backwards a few steps in alarm.

"Nothing," said Zak. "Nothing at all."

"I've had bother with you in the past, you wretched bird," retorted the princess. "Well, you needn't look so smug because I don't want you along either."

"Eh?" Zak cocked his head on one side and his feathers began to bristle with indignation. "Do you mind?" he snapped. "I'll have you know I go everywhere with Sebastian. So there!"

"And I'll remind you as well," hissed the princess, "that this is *my* wish. If it wasn't for me no one would be going anywhere. If I don't want you to come then you won't come. Got it — you miserable old crow? And if you don't like

it, I really will have you shot this time and then you can be hung out in the fields as a reminder to any more of your pals who get above themselves!"

"Well!" spluttered Zak. "I say! Did you hear that, Sebastian? Why, I've never been so insulted in all my life! I'll have you know, you silly creature, if you go on an assignment without me or Maddie, none of the spells will work and you'll probably end up in someone's dungeon for the rest of your life."

"Don't be so stupid," sneered the princess. "Sebastian is perfectly capable of granting a wish on his own . . . aren't you, Sebastian? Tell this mangy bundle of feathers —"

"Don't be so rude!" cried Maddie, entering into the fray at last. She had stayed silent until then but now found she could take no more of this dreadful girl's behaviour, princess or not.

45

"How dare you!" hissed the princess. "I could have you thrown into my father's dungeons for that —"

"Stop!" cried Sebastian and they all jumped. When they were silent he went on. "You are all forgetting one thing. *I* am in charge of this assignment and whatever I say goes. It is entirely up to me who comes along. As it is, you will all come."

"I don't see why." The princess pouted. "You and I would be quite all right on our own, Sebastian. We are only going to find Frederic, after all. He can't be far away because he doesn't have the brains to work out anything too complicated."

So that is what the wish is all about, thought Maddie to herself. The princess didn't really care whether her brother came home or not, she had made the wish simply so that she could have Sebastian all to herself. She had obviously planned it all, knowing that if she made an

important enough wish Zenith would have to proclaim it an official one.

"Things get complicated," said Sebastian firmly. "There's no knowing what we might find out there. I want Maddie with us because for one thing she is brilliant at learning the spells, and Zak proves his worth in all sorts of ways."

"I can learn the spells," said the princess defiantly.

"You can't," said Maddie. "They have to be memorized in Zenith's room and they can't be told to anyone else until they are being used."

"Let's stop this argument right now," said Sebastian sternly. "Either we all go on this assignment and you all accept the fact that I am in charge and my word is final, or we don't go at all and I return the ring to Zenith."

"I'm quite happy with that," said Maddie, glaring at the princess.

"Zak?" said Sebastian.

"Yeah, yeah, I guess," said the raven, nodding his head.

"Your Royal Highness?" Sebastian turned to the princess and they all waited for her reply.

At first Maddie thought she was going to refuse, but then she gave an offhand sort of shrug. "I suppose so," she said. "It doesn't seem as if I have a lot of choice."

"Too right you don't," muttered Zak.

"What did you say?" The princess rounded on the raven.

"Nothing," said Zak. "Nothing at all."

"In that case," said Sebastian, "can we please get on?"

HEY SIS!
HAVING A
GREAT TIME.
I'M NOT COMING
HOME, DON'T
TRY AND FIND
ME! F X

Pigeon Post

PRINCESS LYRA
THE ROYAL
CASTLE
ZAVANIA

Chapter Four

Journey into Zenetzia

"So do you have any idea at all where the crown prince might have gone, Your Royal Highness?" asked Sebastian.

"Not really." The princess shook her head. "He kept sneaking out a lot at night. He thought no one knew, but I did. I caught him a couple of times."

"Didn't Zenith say you'd had a postcard from him?" asked Maddie.

The princess threw her a disdainful glance and for a moment Maddie thought she wasn't even going to bother to answer. Then she gave a shrug. "Yes, I did," she replied at last.

"Do you think we could see it?" asked Sebastian.

"I'll fetch it." The princess turned and went out of the room leaving the friends alone.

"I'm not sure I can put up with too much of her," muttered Zak as the door closed behind her.

"Zak," said Sebastian warningly.

"Well, I ask you. Honestly, she's a pain in the neck! And do we *really* have to say 'Your Royal Highness' every time we speak to her?"

"I suppose so," said Sebastian. "On the other hand, I guess you could just try calling her Lyra and see what happens."

"She'd probably have my guts for garters," said Zak with a snort.

"Well, I'm not going to call her Your Royal Highness," said Maddie firmly. "She's not royal to me. As far as I'm concerned we are talking about two ordinary people who happen to be called Lyra and Frederic."

"Oh boy," chuckled Zak. "I foresee fireworks here . . ." He trailed off as the door opened and the princess came back into the room.

"Here's the card," she said, handing it to Sebastian.

"Hmm," he said as he read it. "Just as Zenith said, all it tells us is that the prince is enjoying himself, that he doesn't want to come home, and that he doesn't want anyone to try and find him."

"Doesn't it give any clue as to where he might be?" Zak flew on to Sebastian's shoulder and peered at the card.

"What's the picture on the front?" asked Maddie.

"Just a picture of the sun," Sebastian replied. "Nothing really out of the ordinary. Who delivered the card?"

"The usual," the princess replied. "Carrier pigeon."

"Maybe that's where we should start," said Sebastian. "Zak, perhaps you could talk to the pigeon. Ask him where he brought the card from."

"OK," said Zak. "I'll go down to the pigeonary and see what I can find out."

"While Zak is doing that," said Sebastian, "maybe we could see the prince's bedroom to see if there are any clues there."

"All right," the princess shrugged, "Follow me."

Maddie and Sebastian followed the princess as she led the way up the grand staircase in the main reception hall, past gilt-framed portraits of her ancestors that adorned the walls, along miles of thickly carpeted corridors, until eventually she

stopped at a room and pushed open the door.

"This is my brother's room," she said. As she glanced around at the huge four-poster bed with its red and silver curtains and covers, the shelves of books, and the vast wardrobes which no doubt contained his clothes, Maddie thought, just for a moment, she could detect a tear in the princess's eye and wondered if perhaps she really did miss her brother after all.

Sebastian wandered around the vast room opening the wardrobe door and each of the drawers of an enormous chest which stood beneath the window. But there were no clues, nothing which gave the slightest indication where the prince might have gone or why.

"Did he have any hobbies?" asked Maddie.

"Only the usual things." The princess shrugged. "He liked to ride his horse. He

53

has a pet falcon . . . nothing out of the ordinary."

"Zenith said there had been problems lately between the prince and your father, the king," said Sebastian hesitantly. "Can you tell us anything about that?"

"Frederic started doing weird things," said the princess.

"We heard about the stud in his nose," said Sebastian.

"And that he'd been dyeing his hair," added Maddie.

"Was there anything else?" Sebastian asked.

"Only that he didn't want to do his royal duties," said the princess. "That made my father really mad. And the more angry he got, the worse Frederic was."

"What about your mother?" asked Maddie.

"Are you referring to the queen?" asked the princess haughtily, then when Maddie

 54

simply nodded, she gave a shrug and said, "She always stands up for Frederic."

"And now that he's gone?"

"She's ill," said the princess. "She's in bed. She just wants to get Frederic back before my father returns. And so do I. I'm sick of doing all Frederic's duties, everything has fallen on me since he went . . ."

So that's another reason she wants him back, thought Maddie. And that reason presented her with the perfect excuse to make a wish that involved Sebastian.

"I don't think we are going to learn any more here," said Sebastian. "Let's go and see if Zak has been able to find anything out from the pigeons."

With a last look round they left the crown prince's bedroom and made their way back to the ground floor where the princess took them out through a rear door into the royal mews.

They found Zak at the far end of the

mews, past the royal horses and the king's falcons, at the centre of an admiring group of pigeons who had formed a circle around him as he strutted up and down showing off.

"Look at that silly bird," scoffed the princess. "Anyone would think he was handsome."

"He is!" Maddie retorted, springing to Zak's defence.

"Well, you would think that, wouldn't you," sneered the princess. "Two odd birds together."

"What do you mean?" demanded Maddie, ignoring the warning hand that Sebastian placed on her arm. "I'm not odd."

"Matter of opinion, I would say," said the princess coolly. "But if anyone was to ask me, I would say that anyone with carrot-coloured hair, freckles and a hideous contraption on their teeth was decidedly odd . . ."

"And you're a horrible bully!" cried Maddie.

"So what?" The princess laughed. "At least I'm beautiful."

"That's only a matter of opinion." With a squawk, Zak flew up out of the circle of pigeons and perched on Sebastian's shoulder.

"Look here, you silly bird —" the princess began, but Sebastian cut her short.

"That's enough," he said sternly. "Zak, have you found out anything?"

"As it happens, yes, I have," said Zak. "That pigeon over there is the one who delivered the card. She was very reluctant

to say anything at first but I exercised my powers of persuasion . . ."

"Yes, all right, Zak," sighed Sebastian, "get on with it . . ."

"It came from a small town in the West called Zenetzia."

"Zenetzia?" echoed the princess.

"Do you know it?" asked Sebastian.

"I've been there once," she replied slowly. "But there's nothing much there. Just a lot of water and boats. I can't imagine what Frederic would want to go there for."

"Well, I guess there's only one way to find out," said Sebastian firmly.

"What's that?" asked Maddie.

"We pay a visit to Zenetzia."

* * *

They left Zavania almost immediately, travelling upriver in a westerly direction in Sebastian's boat. It felt very strange to Maddie to have someone else on board

the boat and even stranger for that someone to be the Princess Lyra. In the past it had only ever been herself, Sebastian and Zak the raven on board. This stretch of the river was also new to Maddie and she watched with interest as they left the reed beds behind and the river broadened and became faster-flowing.

The princess, her golden hair spread around her, lay back on the brightly coloured cushions in the bottom of the boat and languidly trailed her hand in the water while Maddie sat opposite her.

"This is fun," the princess murmured dreamily, lifting her head back and smiling up at Sebastian. "I thought you said these missions are dangerous — I think you've been having us all on. In fact, I think I shall come with you every time you go wish-granting now."

Maddie's heart sank and there came a sound like a muffled snort from Zak, who as always was perched at the front of the boat.

They travelled for a long way until at last Sebastian stopped, resting awhile on the pole and gazing into the distance.

"Zak," he said at last. "Is that it, do you think?"

When the raven remained silent Sebastian spoke more sharply. "Zak!"

"Eh? Eh? What?" The raven stiffened and then flapped his wings.

"He was asleep!" cried the princess. "Fine lookout he turned out to be. He could have led us anywhere. I thought you said he was useful, Sebastian."

"I was not asleep!" declared Zak indignantly.

"So what were you doing then?" sneered the princess.

"I was just resting my eyes," said Zak.

"Huh!" said the princess disdainfully. "Supposing we all did that. Supposing Sebastian had done that . . ."

But Sebastian wasn't listening. Instead he was gazing into the distance with one hand shielding his eyes from the glare of the overhead sun.

"It looks as if Zenetzia is built on the water," he murmured in awe.

"Oh, it is," said the princess airily.

"How do you know?" asked Maddie. She had kept quiet until then, still smarting from the princess's cruel remarks about her appearance and the hated brace she had to wear on her teeth, but now she was interested about the town they were approaching.

"I told you," said the princess, "I've been here before — with my parents as part of a state visit. The town really is built in the water. All the roads are waterways and the people travel everywhere by boat."

"How exciting," said Maddie.

As they approached in silence they saw the town was right where the river met the sea and it seemed to shimmer before them, rising up out of water of the deepest green on which the sunlight danced and sparkled.

"It's beautiful," whispered Maddie, breaking the silence as Sebastian expertly manoeuvred the boat down the wide main waterway of the town. On either side of them vast buildings rose up out of the water, buildings of turquoise, reddish-brown or mustard-yellow, whose colours all blended perfectly together. Other boats had appeared now on the wide waterway, boats all painted a shiny black, similar in appearance to Sebastian's, some carrying passengers but each with a single operator who stood at one end wielding a pole, just as Sebastian did.

Many of the buildings had their own

landing-stages where other boats were moored, lines of them that bobbed and dipped, the waves lapping at their sides. Off the main waterway were many smaller canals that ran between the houses and it was into one of these that Sebastian eventually guided his boat.

It was cooler here and shadowy as the buildings blotted out the light from the sun, but at times it was possible to see inside the buildings through the occasional open shutter, and the friends caught sight of sumptuous rooms breathtakingly lit by crystal chandeliers.

"It's all very grand," whispered Maddie, gazing open-mouthed as they slid noiselessly beneath a series of bridges connecting the buildings around them.

"When we came before, we were guests of the Marquis of Zenetzia and his wife," said the princess smugly.

"I thought you said there wasn't much

here," said Maddie in amazement. "It's beautiful! Absolutely gorgeous!"

"We didn't stay very long," said the princess with a sniff. "We were only passing through as part of our state visit."

"Surely," said Sebastian slowly gazing up at the grand buildings on either side of the canal, "surely if the crown prince was visiting here again he would be received and welcomed by the marquis and his family, as befitted his rank?"

The princess didn't answer and in the end Sebastian leaned forward and said, "Isn't that so, Your Royal Highness?"

"Er, no, not exactly," she replied at last and Maddie thought she sounded rather evasive — as if she didn't really want to discuss that aspect of things.

Sebastian, however, obviously wasn't going to accept that. "Is there something you aren't telling us?" he said at last.

The Princess Lyra shrugged in an off-

hand sort of way. "Not really," she said at last, "it's just that if it was here that Frederic was visiting when he used to go out at night, then I don't think the marquis would have known of his visits."

"You mean his visits weren't official?" asked Zak curiously.

The princess shook her head.

"What makes you think that?" asked Maddie.

"Because when Frederic was getting ready to go out at night," the princess replied, "I know for a fact that he used to go in disguise."

 Chapter Five

Pigeon Post

"What sort of disguise?" asked Zak suspiciously.

The princess hesitated as if she didn't want to answer any question the raven might put to her, then when she realized that the others were also waiting for her reply, she gave a little shrug and said, "He always wore plain, dark clothes, not his usual court finery, and a cloak — he always

wore a dark cloak with a hood."

"Anything else?" said Sebastian.

"No, I don't think so." The princess paused. "Apart from the mask of course."

"Mask?" Sebastian leaned forward. "He wore a mask?"

"Oh, yes, he always wore a mask when he went out late at night."

"Did he have his own boat?" asked Sebastian.

"Boat?" The princess looked up sharply.

Sebastian nodded. "Presumably he must have come here by boat just as we have done."

"No." The princess shook her head. "Frederic didn't have a boat of his own."

"Then how did he get here?" asked Maddie.

"Someone came to get him," said the princess. "I followed him once down to the jetty in the gardens. I had to keep at a distance in case he saw me and by the

time I got there he had gone. I heard the swish of a boat but all that was left were ripples on the stream and the sound of voices in the night air."

"Could you hear what was said?" asked Maddie.

The princess shook her head.

"Did you ever see him come back?" asked Sebastian.

The princess hesitated, then shook her head again. "He must have returned very late but he was always there the next morning . . . until the last time that is, when he didn't come back."

"And you have no idea at all why he was going out?" asked Sebastian.

"There'll be a girl in it," said Zak before the princess could answer. "You mark my words."

"Shut up, Zak," said Sebastian firmly.

"There's always a girl when it's anything like this," Zak went on.

"Well, there might be where you're concerned," snapped Sebastian, "but it doesn't follow that this is the case here."

"Why didn't you tell us all this before?" asked Maddie, staring at the princess in exasperation.

"You didn't ask," the princess replied maddeningly.

"But didn't you think it might be of importance?" Maddie demanded.

"Not really." The princess gave an offhand sort of shrug and when Maddie would have tackled her further Sebastian threw her a warning glance and she bit her lip instead.

They were all silent for a while and then the princess spoke again. "Actually," she said, "there was one time I saw Frederic return. It . . . it was very late at night . . . and . . . and he caught me hiding in the bushes."

"Oh boy!" squawked Zak. "I bet he was happy."

"What did he say?" Sebastian asked, ignoring Zak.

"He was so cross he said that if I told anyone he would tell our father, the king, that I had been bribing the footmen to bring food to my room for midnight parties with my friends."

Maddie looked at the princess with new interest. Midnight parties sounded like fun. But Sebastian looked stern.

"Your Royal Highness," he said, "if we are to grant your wish we really do need to know everything. Now, is there anything else that you haven't told us?"

"No." The princess shook her head. She tried to appear as nonchalant as ever but Maddie suspected she was feeling rather silly.

They carried on in silence through the narrow waterways until the canal opened up again into a wider stretch of water and they came out of the shadows into the

sunlight once more. There was a large jetty before them and Sebastian manoeuvred the boat alongside and with Zak's help moored it to one of the many red and white striped posts sunk deep into the water. Maddie saw with interest that here, alongside the buildings, there appeared to be walkways.

"I suppose," said Sebastian uncertainly, "I suppose that now that we are here we'd better start searching for Frederic."

Maddie glanced sharply at the princess to see her reaction to Sebastian using her brother's name without his title but she remained silent.

"I must confess," Sebastian went on, "I haven't a clue where we should start — does anyone else have any ideas?" He glanced round at the others.

"I've been waiting for you to say that," said Zak.

"You mean you do have an idea?"

Sebastian looked at him.

"Might have," said Zak infuriatingly.

"Well for goodness' sake, tell us then, you silly bird," snapped the princess.

"If you're going to take that attitude . . ." sniffed Zak.

"No one's taking any attitude, Zak," said Sebastian with a sigh. "If you have an idea that might be of help then say so, if not then I suggest you keep quiet."

"I have an address," said Zak.

"Whose address?" asked Maddie eagerly.

"An address the pigeon gave me," Zak answered smugly.

"That was very quick-thinking of you," said Sebastian admiringly. "I'm impressed." He turned to the princess. "I said he has his uses sometimes, didn't I?"

The princess sniffed disdainfully, but Maddie leaned forward with interest. "Whose address is it, Zak?" she asked.

"It's the office where all the post is sorted each day," said Zak. "The pigeon back at the castle told me to go to this address and to ask for Frank."

"And who's Frank?" demanded the princess with a curl of her lip.

"Frank," said Zak, "believe it or not, is the postie who would have collected the prince's card from the postbox wherever he posted it. So if Frank can tell us where that is, we could have some sort of lead as to where the prince might be staying."

"Well, what are we waiting for?" Sebastian jumped from the boat onto the walkway and turned to help the two girls ashore. "Let's go and talk to Frank."

Leaving the boat moored at the jetty they hurried off along the walkway. It seemed very quiet in that part of the town and there was no one about from whom to ask directions, but quite by chance Sebastian happened to glance up.

"Look," he said and clutched Maddie's arm. "Look up there in that window."

They all stopped and looked up, for high above them in one of the buildings a shutter was open and a woman was standing there watching them. She was partly in the shadows, but Maddie could see that she appeared to be a very old woman and was dressed entirely in black with a shawl over her head.

"Excuse me." Sebastian stepped forward and gazed up at the woman. "I wonder if you could help us. We are looking for the sorting office for Zenetzia's postal service."

At first Maddie didn't think the woman had understood what Sebastian had said for she didn't move or speak.

"She doesn't know," said Zak.

"Doesn't want to know more like it," retorted the princess. "Come on, we're wasting time." She turned as if to go.

"Wait," cried Maddie. "Look, I think she's trying to show us."

The old woman had lifted one scrawny arm and appeared to be pointing to a building opposite, a tall, very thin building situated on the far side of the waterway.

"I think she means we are to go over there," said Maddie. "Look, there's a bridge we can cross over."

"Yes, you're right," Sebastian agreed. "Thank you," he called out to the old woman at the same time as sweeping her a bow. The woman nodded in response and, pulling the shutter towards her, fastened it with a loud click.

"Come on," said Sebastian, "let's go and see."

Quickly they sped across the bridge, the two girls following Sebastian while Zak flew low alongside.

Beneath the bridge the water looked dark and deep and somehow dangerous

 75

and Maddie felt herself shudder as she imagined what it would be like to fall in and be swallowed up by the dark water, never to be seen again.

Once on the far side of the bridge, the buildings all looked alike and the friends gazed up in bewilderment.

"I can't see anything that resembles a postal sorting office," said Maddie as images of the office in her home town flashed through her mind.

It was Zak who spotted it in the end. Zak had flown up onto a statue at one end of the bridge and was having a good look around from his vantage point. "There it is," he squawked at last.

"Where?" cried Maddie, Sebastian and the princess all at the same time.

"Up there, right at the top of that building."

"It looks like a pigeon loft to me," said Maddie doubtfully.

"Well, isn't that exactly what it would be?" said Zak.

"Oh," said Maddie. "Yes, I suppose it would." She had quite forgotten, in the heat of the moment, that the postal system they were talking about was run by pigeons.

Together they entered the tall, thin building they had glimpsed from the far side of the bridge. It was so thin that inside it only seemed to consist of a wooden spiral staircase that wound round, up and up.

There were shutters at the various windows that they passed, but shafts of bright sunlight filtered through the wooden slats onto the stairs.

At last they found themselves at the very top of the staircase and in a large loft that looked out on all sides, over the rooftops and chimney pots of Zenetzia.

A team of pigeons were working at a

large wooden bench sorting the dozens of letters, cards and packages that littered its surface and carrying them to the wall at the far end. This wall was covered with pigeonholes, all of which were stuffed with post, waiting to be delivered.

One very plump-chested pigeon turned her head and peered at them over a pair of tiny wire-framed spectacles perched on the end of her beak. "Can I help you?" she demanded bossily.

"I don't think we should say anything about it being the crown prince we are looking for," muttered Sebastian urgently.

"OK," said Zak. "Leave it to me." He strutted across the floor of the loft to speak to the plump pigeon who was obviously in charge.

"Good afternoon!" he said jovially, but the pigeon continued to eye him up and down suspiciously. "We are looking for someone called Frank," Zak went on,

undeterred by the pigeon's attitude.

The pigeon frowned, then turned and with one wing pointed to another pigeon who was pecking at a heap of grain.

"That's Frank," she said. "He's on his lunch break. Frank," she called, "these people are looking for you."

The second pigeon lifted his head and squinted across the floor, straightening up as Zak approached him. "Wotcher mate," he said.

"Hello there," said Zak. "Wonder if you can help us. I'm Zak and these are my friends: Sebastian, who is apprentice to Zenith the WishMaster in Zavania, his friend Maddie, who is from the Other Place, and this is . . . er . . . Lyra, who also lives in Zavania." Zak obviously took great delight in leaving out the princess's title and although she glared at him, she remained silent, almost as if she didn't dare to make an issue of it.

79

Frank nodded. "So what can I do for you?"

"We are on a very important mission," said Zak, puffing out his chest feathers. "We are searching for Lyra's brother, who appears to have gone missing. We know he was recently in Zenetzia because Lyra had a postcard from him."

"Is that a fact?" said Frank. "So how d'you think I might be able to help then?"

It was Sebastian who answered. "We

imagine you must have collected the card and brought it here for sorting before it was delivered. What we are hoping is that you might know where it was posted."

The pigeon stared at them. "You're joking," he said. "Have you got any idea of the amount of mail we get through here each day?"

"Is it a lot?" asked Maddie.

"Is it a lot, she says!" Frank gave a short laugh and turned to another smaller

URGENT!

QUITE QUICKLY PLEASE

TAKE YOUR TIME

WHENEVER

pigeon who was bustling about behind him. "D'ya hear that Sid, the lady asks if we get a lot of mail through here. I ask yer!"

"Maybe you would remember if you saw the card," said the princess. She'd been quiet up until that moment but now she stepped forward and took the postcard that Frederic had sent her out of the pocket of her skirt.

"Wouldn't make no difference," said Frank. "One postcard is much like another . . ." He peered at the card then stopped, drawing his head back in sudden alarm. "Where d'yer get that?" he said, his tone changing as he caught sight of the picture of the sun on the front.

"Didn't you listen?" said the princess haughtily. "This is the card my brother sent me."

"You don't want to know nothing about that," said Frank darkly. As he

spoke, the feathers on the back of his neck began to bristle.

"What do you mean?" demanded the princess. "Of course we want to know about it. This is what he sent."

"Believe you me, luv, you don't want to know." With a shudder that rippled all his feathers, Frank turned away and carried on with his work.

The friends looked at each other.

"What do you think he means?" murmured Maddie.

"Goodness knows," Sebastian replied. "But I don't like the sound of it. Zak," he turned to the raven, "do you think you could find out any more from him?"

"I'll try," said Zak, turning to look at Frank, who had strutted away to the rows of pigeonholes with their letters and cards waiting to be delivered. "But it didn't sound like he wanted to tell us any more."

"It sounded to me as if Frederic may have got himself mixed up in something unpleasant," said Lyra. Even *she* sounded concerned now.

"I'll see what I can do," Zak hopped across to the busy sorting area and tapped Frank on the back of his wing.

The others watched but were unable to hear what the two birds said to each other. At last Zak appeared to give a shrug before hopping back across the floor towards them while Frank went back to his work.

"What did he say?" demanded Maddie and the princess in unison.

"He wouldn't really tell me any more," said Zak.

"What do you mean, he wouldn't tell you any more?" cried the princess. "Does he know who I am?"

"No," said Zak with a snort. "Of course he doesn't know who you are. And I get

the impression that even if he did it wouldn't make a lot of difference."

"What did he say to you, Zak?" asked Sebastian.

"Only more of what he said before," said Zak. "He implied no one should get involved with anything to do with that picture."

"The sign of the sun?" whispered Maddie. "But why? What does it mean?"

"That," said Sebastian grimly, "is what we have to find out."

Chapter Six

The Blue Parrot

They left the sorting office and were standing outside on the walkway, wondering what they should do next, when Maddie heard the flutter of wings behind them. She turned quickly and saw that one of the pigeons had followed them down the stairs.

"Oh," she said. "It's Sid, isn't it?" She had to ask because the pigeons, apart

from the very plump one with the glasses, all looked very much alike.

"That's right." The pigeon spoke in a low tone and kept glancing over his shoulder in a shifty sort of manner as if he really shouldn't be talking to them. "You were asking about that sign?" he said. "The sign of the sun?"

Sebastian nodded. "That's right. Can you tell us anything about it?"

"Can I have a look at it?" Sid muttered.

"Here it is." The princess took the card out of her pocket and showed it to the pigeon. He took one look and drew his head back between his wings just like Zak did when he was disturbed by something.

"What is it?" asked Maddie urgently. "What's the matter with it?"

"It's weird," muttered Sid. "That's what it is. I once knew someone who got mixed up with this and he hasn't been seen since."

"So what does it mean?" asked Sebastian. He sounded bewildered.

"It's an emblem," said Sid. "An emblem for some organization or society or something. I'm not sure which. It's all pretty secret."

"So where does this society meet?" asked Zak. "Can you tell us that?"

The pigeon looked over his shoulder again and at that moment someone called out to him from the top of the staircase behind him.

"I've got to go," he muttered. "I'll be in trouble."

"No, wait," cried the princess as the pigeon turned to go. "You must tell us . . ."

"I'll lose me job . . ."

"Please . . ." implored the princess. "Please . . ."

Sid hesitated and looked at the Princess Lyra standing there with her beautiful golden hair around her

shoulders and with tears gleaming in her large blue eyes.

"All right," he said at last out of the side of his beak. "Try The Blue Parrot, but whatever you do, don't say I sent you." He would have gone then but Zak stepped forward barring his path.

"Hang on a minute, old son," he said. "What is this 'Blue Parrot'?"

"It's a café," said Sid. "It's near where this card was posted. It's down near the Bridge of Tears. Go when it gets dark, but tonight's a festival night, so a word of warning — you'll need to wear masks!"

With that he hopped away, back into the sorting office building and up the spiral staircase.

"Where can we get masks?" asked the princess.

"In a shop?" said Zak. "If we can find any shops, that is."

"I saw some shops," said Maddie

excitedly. "They were down one of those alleyways."

"What about money?" asked Zak.

"I have money," said the princess airily. "I have plenty of money."

"So having a princess with us does have its uses after all," said Zak with a cackle.

"Come on," said Sebastian, sensing another scrap as the princess glared at Zak. "Let's get on with it."

* * *

As it turned out, the shops were full of masks. Masks of every description: big masks that covered the wearer's whole face, little masks that only covered the eyes, masks on sticks, animal masks, sequinned masks, masks made of velvet, of satin, masks for everyone and for every occasion.

By the time the friends had made their purchases and set off for the Bridge of Tears, dusk was falling on Zenetzia.

Maddie had chosen a bright blue mask the same colour as her school uniform, while Sebastian looked even more handsome than usual in his mask of black velvet. The princess had chosen a mask resembling cat's eyes which was edged with tiny sparkling beads.

Only Zak had flatly refused to wear a mask, instead buying a pair of dark, wrap-around sunglasses which gave him a rather sinister look.

"It looks as if everyone is going to the Bridge of Tears," said Maddie as they found themselves caught up in a group of noisy revellers all in fancy dress and wearing masks.

"Sid did say it was a festival night," said Sebastian. "We must keep together," he added. "But if anyone does get lost, make your way back to the boat."

The crowd swept them along amidst much shouting, laughter and singing until

at last Maddie realized they were on a bridge — a very wide bridge which seemed to span the main waterway.

Sebastian called out to a passing group to ask if this was the Bridge of Tears.

"Of course it is!" they shouted back. "The tears of all Zenetzia are washed away beneath the bridge and out to sea."

Maddie stopped and leaned over the stone parapet, intrigued by this idea. The waterway was teeming with boats all packed with masked revellers. The boats, each lit by a solitary lamp, were guided by a single man who manoeuvred his craft with a long pole, and as the boats skimmed the inky blackness of the water, snatches of song drifted up to the watchers who thronged the bridge.

"Oh, it's lovely!" cried Maddie. "It's beautiful and exciting." She turned to the princess. "I can quite understand why Frederic wanted to keep coming here."

They stayed on the bridge for quite a time just watching and enjoying the atmosphere until at last, with a sigh of regret, Sebastian turned away and said, "This is all very pleasant but it isn't getting us anywhere. I think we should press on and find The Blue Parrot." He paused. "Are we all here? Zak?" He turned. "Where's Zak?" he asked.

Maddie looked round. "He's not here," she said.

"Silly bird," sniffed the princess. "He's probably leaned over too far and toppled into the water."

"Oh dear," said Maddie. "You don't really think so, do you?" She peered down into the satiny black water below the bridge.

"They'll find him floating on the top in the morning," said the princess with a snigger.

"Do you know," said Maddie, straightening up and turning to look at

her, "considering you are a princess, you really are the nastiest person I think I have ever met!"

"Maddie . . ." said Sebastian warningly.

"Well, I'm sorry, but she is," said Maddie defiantly. She turned away angrily, only to find her path barred by two figures. "Oh!" she gasped. "Who are you? What do you want?"

The figures, a young man and a girl, both wore long, light-coloured robes and dark masks that covered their eyes. The hoods of their robes were thrown back revealing their hair, which was short and spiky and a curious bright yellow in colour.

"Come with us," said the girl invitingly, reaching out her hand and touching Maddie's arm. "Come to our party."

"We can promise you the most wonderful time of your life," said the man. His voice had a curious lilt to it, almost as if he was singing.

For some reason Maddie suddenly shivered.

"We can't come with you," said Sebastian firmly. "We are waiting for someone."

"Wait a moment," said the princess, suddenly leaning forward and peering first at the man and then at the girl. "Who exactly are you?"

"It doesn't matter who we are," said the girl, with a rippling laugh. "Just come with us and you'll know pleasure like you've never known before . . ."

At that moment the raven suddenly swooped down to join them. "Here's Zak," said Sebastian. "Where have you been?" he added and there was no disguising the relief in his voice.

"Where d'you think I've been?" snapped Zak, lifting his sunglasses and peering with interest at the two robed figures. "While the rest of you have been

95

cavorting about up here, I've been quietly getting on with what we are supposed to be doing, what we came here for . . ."

"Yes, all right, Zak," said Sebastian. "We get the drift. So what have you done?"

"I've made a few enquiries," said Zak. Then he added smugly, "If you care to lean forward a little, over there, to your left, below the bridge structure you will see The Blue Parrot. See it?"

"Oh yes," declared Maddie as she leaned forward. "Yes, there it is. Look Sebastian!"

"Well done, Zak," said Sebastian.

"We'd best get down there then," said Maddie. Straightening up, she turned to the two strangers with the intention of apologizing that they couldn't accept the invitation to their party, but to her surprise the space beside her on the bridge was empty. "Oh," she cried, "they've gone!"

The others turned to look and found that Maddie was right and that the couple had indeed vanished as if into thin air.

"I wonder who they were," said Maddie.

"They looked a bit dodgy to me," said Zak. "That yellow hair didn't look real."

"Didn't you say that Frederic had dyed his hair yellow?" Sebastian asked, turning to the princess.

"Yes . . ." she said and the others could not help but notice that she seemed uneasy about something.

"What is it?" asked Sebastian.

"There was something else," said the princess, "about those two. They both had studs in one side of their noses . . ."

"Also like Frederic," breathed Maddie.

"Yes," the princess nodded, "but there was something else as well, something that I hadn't really thought about before. The studs were very tiny and shaped like the sun."

"And Frederic's?" asked Sebastian.

"The same," said the princess. "Like I said, I never thought about that before."

"What do we do now?" Maddie asked, looking at Sebastian.

"Well, seeing Zak has found The Blue Parrot, I guess we'd better go down there," said Sebastian.

"Actually," said Zak, "there's a bit more to The Blue Parrot than you think."

"What do you mean, more?" said Sebastian as they began to make their way down a steep flight of steps at the side of the bridge.

"You'll see," said Zak over his shoulder.

* * *

It was dim and smoky inside The Blue Parrot Café, very noisy, and crowded with masked revellers sitting at every table, some of whom called out to the friends as they passed and invited them to join them.

Zak led the friends through a beaded curtain to the back room and there, high on a perch shaped like a swing, in front of a huge, gilded mirror was the most magnificent parrot that Maddie had ever seen. Its plumage was the most incredible

shades of blue from the bright sapphire feathers on its back right down to the soft, almost turquoise, downy feathers on its belly.

"This," said Zak importantly, taking off his sunglasses and giving them a little shake, "is Beulah — the Blue Parrot. Beulah is a friend of mine. We go back a very long way, don't we, Beulah?"

"We sure do, kiddo." Beulah the parrot nodded before turning to the others. "You must be Zak's friends. Well, any friends of Zak's . . ." She left the sentence unfinished, instead nodding her head up and down enthusiastically. "I've ordered refreshments for you all."

"That's very kind of you," said Sebastian. "I must admit I am feeling rather hungry."

"How long you had this place, Beulah?" Zak asked, looking round.

"Oh, some time now," said the parrot. "I sold the other place — it wasn't making

enough money. This is great. Between you and me," she leaned towards Zak, "it's a little goldmine, what with all the festivals."

She paused as their refreshments arrived. After they had all sat down round a small table and were tucking into large slices of pizza topped with all sorts of exciting delicacies, and washed down with fizzy lemonade, she went on. "Zak tells me you are looking for someone."

It was Sebastian who answered. "We are looking for a young man called Frederic, who is the brother of our friend, Lyra." He nodded towards the princess. "We believe he may have been visiting your café and may be meeting with a group of people who use the sign of the sun as their emblem . . ."

Without giving him the chance to finish, Beulah gave a loud squawk of rage and almost toppled from her perch.

"What's the matter?" demanded Zak.

"That lot," spluttered the parrot. "They almost got me closed down with their secret meetings. They're a weird bunch, I tell you. There have been all sorts of rumours about their goings-on."

"What kind of rumours?" asked the princess.

"Strange things," Beulah replied darkly.

"We think we might have seen two of them up there on the bridge," said Maddie excitedly. "They acted very strangely and they tried to get us to go to a party with them . . ."

"Oh, they would," said Beulah. "That's how they entice young people."

"They disappeared when they heard Zak mention the café," said Sebastian.

"That figures," said Beulah. "They don't like me anymore."

"Maybe we should have gone with them," said the princess. "Perhaps they

102

would have led us to Frederic. We must try and find them again, Sebastian," she added urgently.

"Oh, if your brother has become one of them he won't be in Zenetzia now," said Beulah, shaking her head. "He'll have long gone, he'll have been taken to their headquarters . . . and if you had gone with them you too would have been drawn in. You mark my words — keep well away from them."

"Sounds spooky," said Zak with a shudder. "So why don't they like you any more, Beulah?" he added, cocking his head on one side as he gazed up at the parrot.

"Well, like I say," said Beulah, "they used to use this place for their meetings . . . and for recruiting their new members . . . and at first, I didn't mind. But recently things seemed to change."

"What do you mean?" asked Sebastian curiously.

"They grew very persistent — it was almost as if someone was telling them to recruit more members . . . or else!" Beulah shrugged. "Anyway, I didn't like their attitude, especially when I heard rumours that the young people they had recruited had never been seen again, so I chucked them out of here and told them in no uncertain terms to find somewhere else. They'd have got me closed down with their shady goings-on — I'd have lost me licence!" Beulah gave an indignant squawk.

"So do you know when their next meeting is?" cried Maddie, clasping her hands together.

"Haven't a clue, sweetie," said the parrot.

"So where do they meet now?" asked the princess.

"Goodness knows." Beulah fluffed out her chest feathers. "But I can tell you where their headquarters are because I

once happened to overhear a couple of them talking."

"And?" said Zak.

"They said something about getting ready for the journey to Sun Mountain."

"Sun Mountain?" Sebastian frowned.

"Do you know where that is?" The princess rounded on him.

Sebastian nodded slowly. "Yes," he said, "I remember Zenith talking of it once. It's actually an extinct volcano and it's in the Mountains of Cloud."

"The Mountains of Cloud?" cried Maddie. "But that's close to where the unicorns have their grazing grounds!"

Sebastian nodded. "That's right," he agreed.

"But that's miles and miles away," Maddie breathed.

"Have you been there, honey?" asked Beulah, eyeing Maddie up and down.

"Oh yes," said Maddie. "We went there

with Peregrine the unicorn when we returned him and his mother Phoebe to their herd."

"Looks like you're going to have to make a return visit," said Beulah. "If you want to find your brother, that is," she added, turning to the princess.

"I hope he's all right," said the princess, and Maddie thought she detected a note of real worry in her voice.

"There's only one problem with making a trip to the Mountains of Cloud as far as I can see," said Zak.

"What's that?" asked the parrot.

"How we get there." Zak paused, then cocked his head in Sebastian's direction. "Time for a bit of magic, would you say, my son?"

"No," said Sebastian thoughtfully. "Not if I can help it. It's far too soon for that."

Chapter Seven

The Return of the Unicorns

"So what then?" asked Zak. "I would have thought magic was the obvious solution — use one of the spells to summon up some transport."

"You should know by now, Zak," said Sebastian, "that I prefer to save the spells in case we need them for some dire emergency."

"Zenith didn't seem to think there

would be anything dangerous in this assignment," said Maddie. "On the other hand I can't say I like the sound of this secret society and of people disappearing."

"Quite," said Sebastian.

"So what are you going to do, sweetie?" asked Beulah.

"I've had an idea," said Sebastian.

"Oh?" Maddie threw him a quick glance and saw that his eyes were gleaming behind the black velvet mask.

"I think the unicorns would help us," Sebastian replied.

"The unicorns?" breathed Maddie, while the princess looked up sharply, a startled expression on her face.

"They said if they could ever help us in any way, they would," Sebastian went on. "I'm sure they would come and transport us to the Mountains of Cloud."

"Oh, wonderful. Brilliant, that is,"

squawked Zak. "But aren't you forgetting one small thing?"

"And what is that?" asked Sebastian calmly.

"Well, I dare say the unicorns would be only too happy to oblige but how do you propose getting a message to them in the first place? Eh? Just tell me that. It's a fair old distance you know."

"Yes, Zak, I know," said Sebastian, "and it's funny you should ask . . ."

Zak stared at him for a long moment, then backing away slightly he said, "Oh no. No. Definitely not."

"It wouldn't take you long, Zak," said Sebastian. "Then while you are gone to fetch them, the girls and I will bring the boat to the mainland to wait for you. And if you are too tired to fly back I'm sure one of the unicorns will let you ride on its back."

"Do you think Peregrine or his mother, Phoebe, will come?" cried Maddie.

"She won't if she knows I'm here," said the princess.

"That's a point," said Zak, eyeing the princess up and down. "And who could blame her?" he added gleefully. "After all, you did try to keep Peregrine in captivity, didn't you?"

"That is all in the past," said Sebastian firmly. "And besides, the unicorns would never, ever bear a grudge against anyone. They are the gentlest of all creatures."

"I don't think you could include the Ice Queen in that," said Zak with a shudder. "Not after what she did to Phoebe."

"The Ice Queen is gone now," said Sebastian. "None of us have any more to fear from her, including the unicorns. Now, Zak, are you going to be on your way?"

"Do I have any choice?" muttered Zak.

"Not really."

"That's what I thought." He flapped

his wings, then peered at Beulah through his dark glasses. "It's been great seeing you again, honeybun," he said out of the side of his beak. "We must get together again some time."

"Sure thing, kiddo," said Beulah, leaning forward and touching his beak with her own. "Take care of yourself. There aren't too many of us old-timers left."

* * *

The festival was still in full swing when Zak took off from the top of the Bridge of Tears. After they had waved him off, Sebastian and the two girls returned to The Blue Parrot Café, where they rested in the back room and snatched what sleep they could until the sun rose over Zenetzia.

After a light breakfast of fruit and hot crusty bread, they bid Beulah farewell and took themselves off in the direction of the jetty, where Sebastian had moored the boat the previous day.

The scene that met their eyes as they crossed the bridge was very different from that of the previous night when the festival had been at its height. People scurried about their business and while there were just as many, if not more boats on the wide waterway as there had been before, there was not one mask to be seen in the early morning sunlight that danced and sparkled on the water.

"Shame really," said Maddie, slipping her mask into her pocket. "I was looking forward to wearing my mask again."

"It was certainly an improvement," said the princess unkindly.

Maddie bit her lip but as she glanced away she caught Sebastian's eye, he smiled at her, and immediately she felt better.

After they had boarded the boat Sebastian drew away from the jetty and guided them down the narrow canal to the main waterway. It seemed in no time at all

they were skimming across the waves towards the mouth of the river, leaving the golden city of Zenetzia behind them shimmering in the early morning haze.

They drew into a deep inlet almost obscured by tall reeds and bullrushes. "This is a bit tricky," called Sebastian. "I can hardly see where we are going."

"I'll help," said Maddie, scrambling to the front of the boat, leaving the princess lying against the cushions with her eyes closed. Calling instructions to Sebastian, Maddie helped him to negotiate the overgrown inlet until at last he was able to moor the boat alongside the bank, where they secured it to the branches of some bushes.

"Yes," said Sebastian. "This is the place. I told Zak we would wait in the shelter of those trees." He pointed to a belt of tall, dark green conifers. "I remembered passing them on our way to Zenetzia."

They climbed ashore and settled down to wait in a field of tall grasses beneath the trees.

"How long do you think he'll be?" demanded the princess after a time. "This is getting boring."

"It's a fair distance to the foothills of the Mountains of Cloud where the unicorns have their grazing grounds," said Sebastian. "It'll take Zak some time to fly there, and then the unicorns will have to get all the way back here. And that's always supposing they'll come," he added.

"It'll be lovely to see Peregrine and Phoebe again," said Maddie, "and Cornelius."

"Who's Cornelius?" asked the princess and Maddie could see she was curious in spite of her earlier indifference.

"Cornelius is Peregrine's father," Maddie replied.

"I'm going to have a bit of a scout

around," said Sebastian, getting to his feet. "You two stay here."

Maddie looked up in alarm. She didn't want to stay anywhere on her own with the princess and would much rather go with Sebastian. But before she could say so, he was disappearing through the trees.

The two girls were silent for a while, then the princess slowly turned to look at Maddie. "How many assignments have you been on with Sebastian?" she asked.

"Two," Maddie replied. "This is the third."

"Why does he always ask you?" The princess wrinkled her nose as if the whole idea was completely beyond her.

"I don't know," Maddie shrugged. "It might be because I've got a good memory and Sebastian has real trouble when it comes to learning the spells."

"I'm amazed Zenith lets you go," said

115

the princess with a sniff. "He's such a miserable old so-and-so."

"No he isn't," retorted Maddie hotly. "I like him."

"You like him!" The princess stared at her contemptuously. "You must be mad. I can't stand him." She paused, then throwing Maddie another curious glance she said, "This Other Place where you come from, what's it like?"

"What do you mean, what's it like?" Maddie frowned.

"Well, is it like Zavania?"

"In some ways." Maddie considered. "And in others not at all."

"What about your people?" asked the princess. "Are they like our people?"

"Yes," Maddie replied slowly. "Yes, I guess they are. There's a girl at the school I go to, her name is Jessica Coatsworth and she is very like you."

"Really?" The princess stared at

Maddie in amazement. "Is she beautiful?"

"Oh yes," Maddie replied. "At least, she thinks she is . . ."

"That's amazing," replied the princess. "I wouldn't have thought there could be anyone else like me."

"I know," said Maddie, her head on one side as she considered the other girl, "it *is* hard to believe, isn't it?"

They fell silent after that as Sebastian

returned, and for a time the three of them dozed in the shade.

It was Maddie who stirred first. A noise had awoken her and at first she wasn't sure what it was, but when the sound grew louder she scrambled to her feet.

"What is it, Maddie?" Sebastian too had opened his eyes and was staring up at her.

"Horses' hooves," she cried, her red curls blowing in the breeze that rippled through the trees and the long grasses. "Listen!"

Sebastian leapt to his feet and, shielding his eyes from the sun, stared into the distance. "It's them!" he cried. "It's the unicorns!"

And suddenly they were galloping through the tall grasses towards them, two magnificent white unicorns with their manes and tails streaming behind them in the wind, while Zak the raven flew alongside them.

"It's Cornelius!" said Sebastian as the

first unicorn slithered to a halt.

"But that isn't Phoebe," murmured Maddie as the second unicorn reared on to its hind legs, pawing the air.

"Hello, my friends!" cried Cornelius. "This is my brother, Conrad. We will be honoured to transport you to the Mountains of Cloud."

"We are very grateful to you," Sebastian replied. "We are on an assignment to grant a wish for the Princess Lyra." Maddie saw Cornelius's eyes roll at the mention of her name. "Her brother, the Crown Prince Frederic, has disappeared," Sebastian hastened to explain, in case the unicorns might be having second thoughts, "and the princess has wished that he would come home."

"Have you any idea where the prince might be?" asked Cornelius, still keeping a wary eye on the princess.

"We've been told that he might have

119

joined a secret society who have their headquarters at Sun Mountain, which we understand is one of the mountains in the Cloud Range near your grazing grounds."

"Yes," said Cornelius. "That is correct. We've heard stories about the people who live on that mountain. It is said they worship the sun."

"And that is where you want us to take you?" asked Conrad.

"Yes, please," Sebastian replied.

"Very well," said Cornelius. "But first, we need to drink, then to rest." Tossing their heads the two unicorns veered away towards the river bank.

"I wonder why Phoebe didn't come," said Maddie as she watched the unicorns canter off.

"She's not well," said Zak, who had flown on to the branch of the tree and was resting his wings.

"What do you mean?" Sebastian looked

up at him. "What's wrong with her?"

"Not really sure," Zak replied. "She's had another foal . . ."

"Oh, how lovely!" cried Maddie.

"But it's more than that." Zak shook his head. "Whatever is wrong with Phoebe is also affecting some of the others in the herd, the older unicorns, and the very young, and anyone who isn't very strong."

"But doesn't anyone know what's causing it?" demanded the princess.

"Cornelius suspects the water," said Zak darkly. "He thinks the stream that they have been drinking from is being polluted."

"How dreadful," cried Maddie. "Whoever would do such a thing?"

"Who indeed," muttered Zak. "You know something, Sebastian old son, something's afoot, believe you me. I can feel it in my bones. There's more going on with this lot than meets the eye."

121

Chapter Eight

The Mountains of Cloud

In a very short while the unicorns returned from the river, where they had drunk their fill, and the friends mounted their backs in readiness for the journey to the Mountains of Cloud. Sebastian and Zak, who was still weary from his long flight, rode on Conrad's back, and the two girls with Cornelius. Maddie would have liked to travel with Sebastian on Cornelius's back just as they had done after they had taken the baby Peregrine back to his family, but for some reason Zak sorted out who was to ride with whom and, for once, nobody argued with him.

As the unicorns moved off through the long, waving grass at a brisk trot, Maddie, who was in front of the princess, leaned forward between Cornelius's ears and spoke softly to him. "Zak says you are worried about your family."

Cornelius turned his head to one side to answer her. "Someone is polluting our water supply," he replied. "I want the herd to move to other, fresher pastures, but too many of them have become so weakened that I fear they would not make the journey."

"Do you know what could be doing this to the water?" asked Maddie.

Cornelius shook his head. "I fear the pollution is coming from high up in the

123

mountains, in the spring at the source of the stream." Then tossing his head, both he and Conrad broke into a canter and any further conversation was lost to the wind.

As Maddie's curls streamed behind her and she held on to the unicorn's horn, the Princess Lyra gave a little shriek of fear.

"Hold on to me," called Maddie.

For a moment nothing happened, as the princess obviously considered it to be beneath her to hold on to Maddie for support, but when the unicorns broke into a full gallop she gave in and, putting her arms around Maddie's waist, clung on for dear life.

Their headlong flight took them into the dark, gloomy depths of the Enchanted Forest where, because of the close proximity of the trees, the unicorns were forced to slow their pace.

Maddie had been here before when she

and Sebastian and Zak had returned Peregrine to his herd. That occasion had been fraught with terror and many dangers as they had struggled to overcome the wickedness of the Ice Queen, and as those memories flooded back, Maddie found the forest no more comfortable now than she had then.

"I d–d–don't l–l–like this place," stuttered the princess over Maddie's shoulder as the unicorns slowed to walking pace.

"No," Maddie replied, "neither do I, but we can't do anything about it."

"But it scares me," the princess retorted.

"Close your eyes then," Maddie replied crisply.

They journeyed on through the blackness of a moonless night until at last, just as dawn was breaking, they emerged from the forest and there, in the far distance, they could see a range of vast

mountains, their peaks surrounded in mist which gave them the appearance of floating in the sky.

"There they are," breathed Maddie, "the Mountains of Cloud."

"I can't believe Frederic is up there," said the princess in her ear. "He doesn't even like heights, for goodness' sake."

"Well, Sebastian said Sun Mountain is in that range," said Maddie. "So if Frederic has indeed gone there with those new friends of his, that is where he is."

"So where are the rest of the unicorns?" asked the princess, craning her neck to see over Maddie's shoulder.

Cornelius heard her and it was he who answered. "They are grazing in the pastures around the foothills," he said.

"Nearly there now," cried Zak as he suddenly flew up from Conrad's back. He was still wearing the sunglasses he had bought in Zenetzia and he looked so

funny that Maddie had to fight back a sudden fit of the giggles.

The unicorns cantered on through fields of fresh green grass dotted with poppies and large white daisies, until at last a shout from Sebastian told the others they had arrived.

"There they are," he cried, pointing ahead, his cloak billowing behind him. "The unicorn herd!"

The unicorns were grazing quietly in the misty shelter of a belt of trees, some in groups, others singly, but they all looked up and whinnied in greeting at the return of Cornelius and Conrad.

Maddie and the friends dismounted, stiff from their journey, to find that Peregrine had left the rest of the unicorns and was trotting across the grass to meet them.

"Peregrine!" cried Maddie, opening her arms wide as the little unicorn broke

into a canter then, as he reached her, wrapping her arms around his neck and hugging him tightly. "How lovely it is to see you again."

"Maddie! Sebastian! Zak!" Tears were running down Peregrine's face in his excitement at seeing his friends again but then, as they all petted and made a great fuss of him, he happened to turn his head and caught sight of the princess. Immediately his ears flattened against his head and he rolled his eyes.

"It's all right, Peregrine," said Sebastian quickly. "Really it is."

"But it's her . . ." whimpered Peregrine. "She tried to keep me in captivity . . ."

"I know," said Sebastian while the princess sniffed in contempt before tossing her head and looking away. "But she's sorry now, aren't you?" He turned to the princess, but she ignored him.

"Aren't you, Your Royal Highness?"

Sebastian said again, more loudly.

"What?" The princess turned at last and looked down her nose at Sebastian.

"Sorry that you kept Peregrine in captivity?"

"Yes, yes," she snapped impatiently, "I suppose . . ."

"There you are, you see?" said Sebastian, turning back to Peregrine who, although he nodded, looked far from sure and, Maddie noticed, continued to keep a safe distance from the princess.

"Why are you here?" asked Peregrine curiously as they began to walk across the grass to the rest of the herd beneath the trees.

"We are looking for the princess's brother, Prince Frederic," Sebastian explained. "We believe he may be somewhere in this area."

"Well it's wonderful to see you all again . . . Did you know we have a new foal?"

"Yes." Maddie smiled. "Can we see her?"

Peregrine nodded. "She's over there with my mother. Her name is Chloe."

After thanking Conrad, who went off in search of his own family, and together with Cornelius and Peregrine, the friends made their way to the band of trees where they found Phoebe with her new daughter.

Phoebe was delighted to see the friends again and was proud to show them her foal, who was only a few days old and still very unsteady on her long legs. However, it soon became apparent that many of the unicorns, including Cornelius's family, were very weak. Their coats had become dull and had lost their beautiful glossy sheen and many of them found difficulty in standing for very long and were experiencing severe stomach cramps.

"Why didn't you send for us to help

130

you?" said Sebastian. "Why didn't you appeal to Zenith? Why didn't you make a wish?"

"I thought I could move them myself in time," said Cornelius. "It was such a gradual thing, you see. And I only suspected it might be the water that was responsible on the day that Zak came to get us."

"And yet still you came to help us even though you were in such trouble yourselves," said Maddie with tears in her eyes.

"We told you we would always be here if you needed our help," Cornelius replied proudly.

"Well we are here now," said Sebastian firmly. "And you need *our* help."

"Are we talking a spell here, old son?" asked Zak, cocking his head to one side.

"Absolutely," Sebastian replied. "If

that is what it takes. But first, I would like to see the stream."

"Very well," Cornelius replied. "I will take you there."

While Sebastian and Cornelius were gone the others rested with Phoebe, Peregrine and Chloe, and Maddie explained to Phoebe why they were there. Just like Peregrine, Phoebe also seemed wary of the princess.

"You can't blame 'em," muttered Zak to Maddie when she quietly commented as much to him, "not after all the grief she caused them."

In a very short while Cornelius returned with Sebastian riding on his back.

"What's the score, old son?" asked Zak.

"The stream is indeed polluted," said Sebastian grimly. "The water is a strange yellowy colour. It tastes metallic and it has a strong smell of sulphur about it. It's no wonder it's been making the unicorns ill."

 132

"It wasn't so bad to start with," said Cornelius. "In fact for a long time we didn't even know there was anything wrong with it."

"What do you think is causing it?" asked Maddie anxiously.

"Goodness knows," Sebastian replied. "But whatever it is, I intend to put a stop to it. Once the unicorns have pure, fresh water to drink again I think they will slowly regain their strength. I intend to use one of our spells to bring that about. Does everyone agree?"

"Oh yes!" cried Maddie.

"Absolutely, old son!" squawked Zak, waggling his sunglasses.

"Right," said Sebastian. "Now . . ."

"Wait a minute!" The princess suddenly jumped to her feet and stood, hands on hips, glaring at the others. "Are you saying you intend using one of your spells just to de-pollute that stream?"

"That's right," said Sebastian quietly.

"D'you have a problem with that?" asked Zak, eyeing the princess up and down.

"As it happens, yes I do," the princess retorted. "Exactly how many spells do you have to grant my wish?"

"Just the two," said Zak with obvious relish.

"I wasn't talking to you, you mangy creature," snapped the princess, while Peregrine rolled his eyes and gave a nervous whinny, and Zak gave a squawk of indignation.

"It's true," said Sebastian calmly. "We do only have the two spells . . ."

"Then I demand that you keep them both to use on my wish," said the princess with her eyes flashing.

"But the unicorns are in trouble!" cried Maddie scrambling to her feet.

"So might Frederic be in trouble!" retorted the princess.

"The unicorns are our friends!" cried Maddie.

"And Frederic is my brother!" The princess turned sharply. "Sebastian, you are in charge of this assignment — or so you keep telling us — so it's up to you to tell the unicorns that the spells will not be wasted in this way."

"Oh boy!" Zak put his head under his wing. "I said she'd be trouble," he muttered. "Didn't I say she'd be trouble?"

By this time Sebastian had drawn himself up to his full height and, flicking his black cloak over his shoulder, he said, "You are quite right, Your Royal Highness. I am in charge of this assignment, and whatever I decide, will be done."

Just for one second Maddie's heart sank as she imagined that the princess was about to get her own way, then her spirits soared as Sebastian stepped forward and, beckoning for her to join him, lifted his

hand so that the rays of the early morning sun caught the topaz stone in the ring he wore on his finger.

Maddie took a deep breath and together she and Sebastian, watched by Zak, the princess, and the entire unicorn herd, began to recite the words of the spell.

"Zaroosza Zariskin Zarene
Zollaria Zolluria Zadaz
Bring Amber Light Serene
In the Glow of this Topaz."

Everything was still and silent after they had finished and for a moment Maddie wondered if anything was going to happen. Usually after a spell was spoken there was a blinding flash from the stone in the ring that Sebastian wore.

And then, very gradually, the friends became aware of a golden glow that seemed to settle on the mountains and

136

the pastures, lighting not only the sky but bathing the very earth in its gentle light.

Then in a loud voice Sebastian said, "By the Power of the Topaz let the stream flow forevermore with fresh pure water."

The light grew even brighter and everyone gazed around in wonder, until the glow faded and the whole area returned to the soft pastel colours of a normal summer's morning.

"You will find," said Sebastian, his voice quiet but full of confidence, "that the water from the stream is perfectly safe to drink once more."

"We will never be able to thank you enough for this," said Cornelius, his voice breaking with emotion as the rest of the herd began to move towards the stream. Their thirst was making them frantic for water.

By this time tears were running down Phoebe's cheeks as she nuzzled her foal,

Zak was sniffing loudly, Maddie gulped to try to get rid of the lump in her throat, and even the princess seemed overawed and was silent.

"And now," said Sebastian, his voice full of authority, "we must move on and fulfil our obligation. Our destination, Sun Mountain, is in the midst of the mountain range and it is there that we believe we will find the Crown Prince Frederic."

"I can guide you through the foothills and up as far as the pass that goes through the mountains," said Cornelius. "After that I fear I will not be able to help you as the path is too narrow and too steep for unicorns."

"We will be grateful for any help you are able to give us," said Sebastian.

"I guess what he really means," whispered Zak to Maddie, "is that with only one spell left we are going to need all the help we can get."

Chapter Nine

Hamish McTavock

The path into the mountains was steep, narrow, and very rocky and the friends found it took every ounce of their concentration to prevent themselves from losing a foothold and plunging over the side.

"This is as far as I can take you," said Cornelius at last. "Over there in the distance you can see Sun Mountain but

you have a long way to go yet to get there."

They all looked towards the distant mountain whose summit was eerily wreathed in mist.

"Thank you for your help," said Sebastian. "We will see you again on our return."

"Take care of yourselves," said Cornelius, then with a whinny and a toss of his head he was gone, picking his way carefully back down the narrow path.

The friends trudged on up the steep mountain pass until eventually the princess began to complain. "I'm tired, I'm hungry and I'm thirsty," she declared bitterly. "I want somewhere to rest, I want some cake to eat, and some fruit juice to drink."

"And I suppose you think you're just going to find a transport café round the next bend," said Zak with a snort.

"Of course not," the princess replied coldly. "But Sebastian has magic. Surely

that's the whole point of him having magic spells, for things like this, and if he can do one for those unicorns, then he can do one for me."

"Just for you?" cried Maddie indignantly, throwing herself down onto a patch of grass beneath a large rock that jutted out above them. "What about the rest of us?"

"You're not a princess. I am!" Lyra retorted.

"Well, if that's the way a princess behaves then I'm glad I'm not one," declared Maddie. Her face was red and shiny, her curls tangled by the wind, and she was quite out of breath after their long climb. As the others flung themselves down on the piece of grass beside her, she couldn't help but notice that Sebastian looked a bit worried and she wondered if he too was concerned about what they were going to eat and drink.

It had taken them nearly all morning to

climb up to the pass through the mountains and they had no way of knowing how much further they had to go, for Sun Mountain seemed as far away as it had when they had first set out. Maddie knew there was no way that Sebastian would want to use the remaining spell so soon. He would want to keep that just in case they faced any life-threatening situations.

"We'll rest awhile here," said Sebastian firmly.

They sat gazing out at the mountains all around them until at last Sebastian pointed to the peak of Sun Mountain which was now visible through the mist. "Look Zak," he said, "there are birds flying up there, what do you think they are?"

"Dunno," said Zak, shaking his head. "Probably eagles up as high as that."

"There are hundreds of them," said Maddie. "They don't look big enough to be eagles."

"I can't imagine what Prince Frederic is doing up here," said Sebastian.

"I was thinking the same thing," Maddie replied. "I think he must be here because he doesn't have any choice."

"You mean he is being kept against his will?" cried the princess, her voice shrill in the thin air on the mountainside.

"Well, I can't imagine anyone choosing to be up here, can you?" retorted Zak. "And from what Beulah said, it certainly sounded as if people were being brought here against their will."

"But if that's the case, why would Frederic have said in his card that he was quite happy and that he didn't want to come home?" demanded the princess.

"Maybe he was happy when he wrote it . . . or maybe someone forced him to write it," said Zak with a shrug. "I don't know . . . it's no good asking me . . ."

"What's that noise?" said Maddie,

suddenly looking over her shoulder.

"What noise?" said the princess. "I can't hear anything."

"Yes, listen, there *was* a noise," Maddie insisted. "There it is again. Listen."

They all stopped then and listened, and sure enough, there was a noise. A strange, chomping noise and it seemed to be coming from the rock above them.

"It sounds like someone chewing . . ." Maddie scrambled to her feet and peered up on to the rock.

As she did so a head suddenly appeared over the top of the rock. It was surrounded by wispy white hair and a long, straggly beard. As the chewing stopped, pale blue eyes stared at them from beneath a pair of beautifully curled horns. Between the horns a tartan beret with a red pom-pom rested at a rakish angle.

"Oh!" exclaimed Maddie in amazement. "It's a goat!"

"A goat?" cried the animal in contempt. "Are you calling me a goat?"

"Well, aren't you a goat?' demanded Maddie.

"Of course it's a goat," said the princess, turning away, bored.

"I'll have you know," spluttered the animal, "I'm not just any old goat. I happen to be Hamish McTavock — Laird of the Mount, Guardian of the Pass, Protector of . . ."

"Yes, quite," said Sebastian hastily. "We are very sorry to have disturbed you, Mr McTavock . . ."

"Hamish will do. Hamish will do," the goat replied, eyeing them all balefully from under his shaggy, white eyebrows. "So who are ye all? And what are ye all doing on my mountain pass? It gets more like a main line station up here every day, I can tell ye that. I came up here to live to get away from it all and I tell ye, I've had

145

more people pass me by than I ever saw in my last abode."

"I'm sorry about that." Sebastian stood up. "I'm Sebastian, I'm Apprentice to Zenith the WishMaster and these are my friends, Maddie, Zak and the . . . er, Lyra."

"Yes, yes, yes," said Hamish the goat irritably. "But what are ye doing up here? That's what I want to know."

"We are searching for Lyra's brother," said Sebastian.

"And ye think you're going to find him up here?"

"Well, we've been informed . . ." Sebastian began to explain but Zak cut him short.

"You said something about a lot of people passing through," he said, squinting up at Hamish through his sunglasses.

"Aye, that's right. Morning, noon and night they've been to-ing and fro-ing."

"But where are they going?" asked Maddie.

"Over there." Hamish turned and nodded towards the distant mountain.

"You mean Sun Mountain?" said Sebastian. "Why would all these people be going there?"

"Ye don't want to know about that place," said Hamish darkly. "Believe me, ye don't want to know."

"But we do," cried Maddie. "We believe that is where we have to go."

"Aye well, don't say I didna warn ye." Hamish waggled his beard then went on. "Well, it's a weird lot up there and no mistake. They belong to a cult who call themselves People of the Sun. Ye can see them up there at sunrise and again when it sets, bowing down and chanting their weird songs. They come through here on their way out and then they bring others back with them."

"And has that always happened?" asked Sebastian. "Have these People of the Sun always lived up there on the mountain?"

"Aye, they have," Hamish replied. "And they've always gone out to get more members for their cult, but lately things have changed," he went on darkly. "And changed for the worse if ye ask me."

"What do you mean?" asked Maddie breathlessly.

"I heard a rumour from a skylark that the cult's goddess has arrived and it

sounds as if she's shaken 'em all up," said Hamish with a snort.

"In what way?" asked Sebastian, leaning forward with interest.

"Well, for a start, she's stepped up the recruitment drive, aye she has that an' all," muttered Hamish. "I told ye, traipsin' through here morning, noon and night they are. And there's another thing, it's only since this goddess of theirs has been on the scene that the water in the stream isn't fit to wash your feet in, let alone to drink! The skylarks weren't too happy about that, I can tell ye, and I've been reduced to sucking dew from the ferns."

"The unicorns didn't think it was a bundle of fun either," said Zak. "What caused it, old chap, any idea?"

"Goodness knows!" said Hamish with another snort. "Rumour has it she's been polluting the water with her magic potions . . . They've got their own well on

the mountain so they were all right . . . But for the rest of us . . . !"

"It's all right now," Maddie cried. "Sebastian has got magic and he's used a spell to make the water fresh and clean again."

"Eh?" Hamish stared at Sebastian as if he was seeing him for the first time. "Is that a fact?"

"Tell me," said the princess slowly, "what happens to the people that are brought here to Sun Mountain — do they just become members of the cult?"

"They used to." The goat shrugged. "But rumour has it that since this goddess of theirs has arrived, she's put them all to work building her a temple facing the rising sun. The truth is," Hamish lowered his voice, "no one ever sees these folk again."

"Oh dear," said Maddie with a shiver. "That's what Beulah said, and Sid the pigeon. Do you know, my arms have gone

all goosepimpled just thinking about it."

"What are those birds, old chap?" asked Zak, peering into the distance where the birds could still be seen flitting back and forth around the summit of Sun Mountain.

"Bats," Hamish replied. "Thousands of 'em. Pesky little varmints. Again, I've heard tell they guard her, the Sun Goddess — they're her personal bodyguard."

"I thought bats only came out at night," said Maddie.

"Not this lot," the goat replied. "Flitting about morning, noon and night they are."

"I don't like bats," said the princess with a shudder. "I always think they will get tangled up in my hair."

"I think they are quite sweet really," said Maddie. "All soft and furry."

"I don't think ye will find this lot very sweet," said the goat. "They aren't the soft and furry kind."

"What do you mean?" asked Zak warily as the friends all gazed towards the summit of Sun Mountain.

"These are Devil Bats," said Hamish. "Vicious little brutes they are an' all." He chuckled suddenly and they all turned to look at him. "So are ye still wanting to go on this trip of yours to Sun Mountain?" he asked.

"We have to," Sebastian answered for them all. "We have an assignment to carry out."

"Well, rather ye than me," the goat replied with a sniff. "But before ye go, ye'd best rest awhile. There are plenty of berries on the bushes for ye to eat, and if the water from the stream is as fresh as ye say it is, then ye won't mind being the first to drink it."

Rested and refreshed, the friends eventually left Hamish McTavock, with many a dire warning ringing in their ears, and carried on their way to Sun Mountain.

"It's very quiet," said Maddie, when they finally reached the base of the mountain and began climbing once more. "I can't even see any of those bats now."

"Good thing too," said the princess with a sniff. "I didn't like the sound of them."

"Can't say I like the sound of any of it," retorted Zak. "There's something about this whole thing that is beginning to stink . . . but I can't quite put my feather on what it is."

"It reminds me of something," said Maddie slowly.

"What do you mean?" Sebastian threw her a sharp glance.

"I don't know. I'm not sure." Maddie shook her head. "It just feels like something else. Some other time and some other place . . . but I can't quite think what."

"I wonder where this temple is that the Sun Goddess is having built?" said Zak,

peering up at the sheer face of Sun Mountain that towered above them.

"That old goat said it faced the rising sun," said the princess.

"Which means it must be around the other side of the mountain," replied Sebastian thoughtfully. "Zak, why don't you fly around there and see if you can see anything?"

"Why is it always me that has to do these things?" grumbled Zak.

"Because you are the only one who can fly," said Maddie.

"Huh!" Zak hunched his shoulders.

"Off you go," said Sebastian, "but be careful. And whatever you do, watch out for the Devil Bats."

"You don't think I'm scared of a handful of flying mice, do you?" retorted Zak contemptuously.

"Of course not," said Maddie soothingly. "But be careful anyway."

"We'll carry on climbing," said Sebastian as Zak flapped his wings a few times and took off, flying into the path of the sun.

"I hope he'll be all right," said Maddie anxiously.

"Why shouldn't he be?" The princess gave a shrug. "He's always going on about how clever he is. Now's his chance to prove it."

"I've just got a feeling, that's all," said Maddie.

"What is it, Maddie?" Sebastian, who was a little way ahead of the two girls, stopped and turned to look down at them.

"I don't know," said Maddie. "I just feel something is very wrong. In spite of the fact that Zenith said he thought this assignment would be perfectly straightforward I feel we could be walking into great danger."

Chapter Ten

Sun Mountain

The base and sides of Sun Mountain were almost concealed by bushes and thick foliage, and as the friends scrabbled up the rocky path scraping their knees and hands, sharp thorns tore at their clothes while the overhead sun beat mercilessly down.

"I don't like this," wailed the princess at last. "I want to go home."

"We all do," snapped Maddie, "and if it

wasn't for your brother going off with this weird lot that's where we would be."

The princess was silent after that, but it was obvious she was finding the going very tough until, just when they were all beginning to wonder how much further they could go, there suddenly came the loud sound of wings whirring overhead.

"Zak!" cried Maddie hopefully, shielding her eyes from the glare and gazing up into the sky.

"Well, let's hope he's found something out . . ." grumbled the princess.

"It isn't Zak!" gasped Sebastian, suddenly clutching the arms of the two girls and pulling them into the gorse bushes against the face of the mountain. "It's the bats!"

And indeed it was. In a dark cloud, thousands of them of all shapes and sizes with sharp, pointed wings, ugly, squashed faces and evil, vicious-looking teeth.

Swooping and screeching — a weird, high-pitched sound — they swept past the spot where the friends hid crouching in the bushes and clutching each other in terror.

Maddie felt sure they would be discovered at any moment and that the bats would attack them but to her amazement they appeared not to realize that the friends were there, sweeping past them and disappearing around the mountain.

"They've gone!" cried Sebastian at last in relief. "I really thought we were in trouble then. I only hope Zak doesn't bump into them."

"Sebastian, look at this!" The princess, who had been closest to the sheer rock face of the mountain, suddenly clutched at the sleeve of Sebastian's shirt.

"What is it?" Sebastian peered through the thick foliage to where the princess was staring.

"There's an opening here," she said

excitedly. "It's a sort of doorway — do you think it's a cave?"

"There's only one way to find out — come on," said Sebastian, and crouching low he led the girls through the narrow opening in the side of the mountain.

"But what about Zak?" asked Maddie anxiously.

"He'll find us," said Sebastian over his shoulder.

"If it is a cave, it's a very deep one," said Maddie in a small voice after they had been walking and still climbing for some time. "It seems more like a passage and it's going right into the mountain."

"I think you are right." Sebastian's voice sounded tight with excitement. "And there's something else," he went on. "If Sun Mountain really is an extinct volcano like Zenith said, then it probably would be hollow."

"I hope that doesn't mean it's going to

erupt at any moment," said Maddie nervously.

"Of course it won't," sneered the princess. "Not if it's extinct, stupid. Honestly, don't you know anything?"

Maddie bit her lip and glanced at Sebastian for support, but he didn't appear to be listening. He had gone on a little ahead of the two girls and suddenly he stopped. "I say," he gasped. "Come and have a look at this!"

The girls caught him up, then they too simply stood and stared. The stone pathway had opened up into an enormous cavern and the friends found themselves perched right on the edge of a very narrow ledge that seemed to run right round the sides of the huge void.

"I was right," breathed Sebastian. "The mountain is hollow — this is the crater which must have formed in the days when the volcano was erupting . . ." Leaning

forward, he peered over the edge and for one awful moment it seemed as if he might plunge over the side.

"Be careful, Sebastian!" cried Maddie, reaching out to grab a handful of his cloak and holding on tightly to it.

But Sebastian was intent on peering down into the very depths of the mountain far below them. "Down there," he went on, his voice echoing in the vast chamber, "must be the remains of the volcano."

Maddie and the princess peered cautiously over the edge, but all they could see was a dark, yawning chasm beneath them.

"There's someone coming!" It was the princess's turn to sound the alarm.

"Is it those bats again?" Nervously Maddie peered across the crater.

"No, it isn't the bats. Look, it's people!" The princess pointed and, sure enough, a line of people were climbing up

a flight of steps that appeared to ascend from the very depths of the crater. They were dressed in creamy-coloured cloaks, their hoods drawn up right over their heads so that they partly obscured their faces, and as they moved they chanted a dirge in a low, monotonous tone.

"Who are they?" whispered Maddie.

"At a guess I would say they are the People of the Sun," Sebastian murmured. "But, whoever they are, I don't think it would be a very good idea to let them see us."

"But they are coming this way," hissed the princess as the first figure in the line reached the top of the steps, turned, and began to walk along the ledge in their direction.

"We need to hide," said Sebastian, looking frantically around.

"There were boulders," said Maddie, quickly looking over her shoulder. "Back there."

The boulders were just inside the passage that the friends had come through, almost at its very mouth. "Come on," said Sebastian. "Quickly, we could be in all kinds of danger if they see us."

"You still have the spell," whispered the princess urgently, as the friends crouched behind the boulders, waiting in fear and trepidation as the line of chanting, hooded figures grew closer.

"I don't want to use that until we have to," Sebastian muttered back. "We could well need it to get out of this place . . ." He trailed off. As the first of the line drew level with the entrance of the passageway he appeared to be holding his breath.

Maddie's heart was thumping so loudly it seemed to be keeping rhythm with the chanting, and as she squeezed her eyes tightly shut she felt certain it would be heard.

Finally she heard Sebastian let go of his

breath in a great sigh of relief and she dared to open her eyes once more and to look up.

"They are going by," he whispered. "For one awful moment I thought they were going to come into the passage."

The line of figures were filing one by one past the entrance to the passageway, until at last they were all gone and Sebastian crawled forward.

"Thank goodness for that," Maddie whispered, then realized that in their fright she and the princess had clasped each other's hands. "It's all right — they've gone now," she added, embarrassed now as they loosened their grip on each other.

"But for how long ? That's what I'd like to know," said the princess.

At that moment Sebastian crawled back to the two girls. "They're following the ledge right round this side of the crater," he said. "Come and see . . ."

They cautiously followed him and, sure enough, they could see the white-robed column as it filed around the ledge.

"They're climbing now," whispered Maddie as the figures appeared to be moving up another flight of steps. Then, even as the friends watched, the column seemed to disappear before their very eyes.

"Oh," said Maddie. "They've gone. They've vanished!"

Even their whispers sounded loud and seemed to echo right around the walls of the crater.

"I want to follow them," said Sebastian. "I want to see where they have gone."

"Do we have to?" said the princess with a shudder.

"You two can stay here if you want to," said Sebastian.

"No," Maddie replied quickly, "I'm coming with you." Turning to the princess she said, "I thought you wanted to find

Frederic — you won't find him sitting here."

"All right." The princess screwed up her face. "I suppose I'll have to come with you."

Together they crept around the ledge, all the while alert for any sound that might herald the approach of danger either from bats or humans, but they reached the far side of the crater without further mishap.

"Well," said Sebastian running his hands over the rough surface of the walls, "I'm sure this is the spot where they disappeared."

"But where could they have gone?" said Maddie in bewilderment.

"They can't just have vanished into thin air," muttered Sebastian. "There must be another opening here just like the one we came through." He stopped a moment later and gave a little grunt of satisfaction. "Yes, here it is. Just as I

thought. It's very narrow, but it's an opening."

"Where do you think it leads?" whispered the princess, her eyes now wide with fright.

"I've no idea," Sebastian replied. "But I guess there's only one way to find out. Come on, follow me." Taking a deep breath, he slipped into the almost concealed opening in the rock and after a moment's hesitation the two girls followed him.

It was dark in this passage, much darker than it had been in the other one. It was much narrower and there were steps leading upwards. As they climbed, it grew a little lighter, until at last they turned a corner and without warning a sudden glare of light attacked their eyes.

"We've come right through the mountain," gasped Maddie. "We must be on the other side."

They stood there blinking in the heat from the fierce rays of the sun, struggling to adjust their eyes to the sudden contrast from the gloom within the passage.

The princess seemed to recover first and it was she who was the first one to look down. As she did so she gave a shriek of pure terror.

"What is it ... ?" Maddie began in alarm, then she too looked down — but there was nothing that could have prepared her or the others for what they saw.

They were on another ledge, one even narrower than the last, and immediately below them was a sheer drop right down the side of the mountain. As her tummy seemed to do a somersault Maddie gasped and closed her eyes.

"Look!" Sebastian's breathless command forced her to open her eyes again and to follow his gaze.

The ledge they were on came to an

168

abrupt halt at the head of yet another flight of steps leading down on to a flat plateau on the very edge of the mountain itself, where, facing the sun, the most beautiful building that Maddie had ever seen was in the process of being built.

It was constructed of great blocks of stone that were being hewn from the mountainside itself. Before each block was lowered into place it was dipped in

vast vats filled with a substance that looked like molten gold. The overall effect of the golden building was so dazzling that it was impossible to gaze at it for very long.

"I've never seen anything like it," breathed Sebastian.

"Who do you think it belongs to?" whispered Maddie.

"It must be the temple of the Sun Goddess that Hamish McTavock told us about," he replied.

"Look at those men!" said the princess suddenly.

There were a lot of people on the plateau. Some were robed in the long, hooded cloaks that the friends had seen before, but there were others, young men and boys clad only in loincloths or tattered trousers, who had no protection either on their backs or their heads from the blistering heat of the sun. Even

worse was the fact that these poor wretches, as they toiled in the noonday heat hewing out the stone from the face of the mountain, were shackled together at their ankles by cruel metal chains.

"Oh!" cried Maddie. "Those poor, poor boys!"

Suddenly the princess gripped Maddie's hand again and when Maddie turned to look at her she saw that the other girl's eyes were wide with shock.

"What's the matter?"

"There!" The princess lifted her hand and pointed. "There he is — there's Frederic! He's one of them!"

Maddie squinted at the robed figures, some who were standing together in groups, others who were kneeling or bowing down to the sun. "How do you know?" she asked. "They all the look the same to me in those robes."

"No, no," cried the princess, clearly

very distressed now. "You don't understand, Frederic isn't one of those. That's him there . . ." She pointed to one of the boys in chains in the gang. His hair was a sort of faded yellow with the darker regrowth showing through. Like the others he wore tattered trousers and his back and feet were bare.

"Oh surely not." Maddie was shocked. "Frederic's a prince. He wouldn't be . . . would he?"

She stopped and stared again. "His postcard said he was well and happy and that he didn't want to come home. He can't be happy doing that. No one would be."

"That card was sent from Zenetzia," said the princess. "Before he got here to Sun Mountain. Oh, Sebastian!" She turned imploringly. "Look at him! Oh, poor Frederic! You have to rescue

him . . . you have to do something!"

But Sebastian wasn't listening. Instead he was staring at the figure of a woman who had just emerged onto a balcony on the completed section of the temple. "Look!" he breathed. "That must be her — the Sun Goddess!"

Chapter Eleven

The Sun Goddess

She was dressed in robes of gold that with her every movement shimmered and shone in the sunlight. On her head she wore a huge headdress, also of gold, shaped like the sun with its rays encrusted with precious stones. As Maddie and Sebastian stared at her she lifted her face to the sun and opened her arms wide as if embracing its very warmth.

It was Sebastian who finally put the awful possibility into words.

"It's her!" he said, his voice barely more than a hoarse whisper.

"It can't be!" Maddie replied, her voice trembling. "She's gone."

"We thought she'd gone," muttered Sebastian. "But she did swear she'd return."

"But how could she have made such a comeback . . . ?" Maddie threw out one arm in a sweeping gesture to encompass the golden temple and all the activity on the plateau. "She had nothing . . ."

"She's ruthless, evil and she still had her magic . . . inferior as it is," Sebastian replied slowly.

"Would someone mind telling me what is going on?" demanded the princess and the other two turned and looked at her as if they had completely forgotten she was there.

"Who is she?" she demanded curiously.

"That woman, the Sun Goddess . . . who exactly is she?"

"That," said Sebastian grimly, "believe it or not, is the woman who used to call herself the Ice Queen."

While Maddie caught her breath at the very sound of that evil name, the princess frowned. "How can it be?" she demanded. "I understood she fled after she lost her army and her Ice Palace."

"So she did," Sebastian replied. "Somehow she appears to have staged a comeback."

"I said all this reminded me of something," said Maddie slowly. "The people taken away and forced to work and then never seen again . . ." She shuddered. "It's like it was before . . . only then she had her Ice Soldiers to help her . . . and this time she has . . ."

"This myterious cult of the People of the Sun," said Sebastian. "I wonder how

she has persuaded them to do her will."

"By force, I should think," said the princess.

"I don't think so," said Sebastian, slowly leaning forward and peering over the ledge again. "It's the others who are in chains, not the Sun People."

"So how are we going to rescue Frederic?" asked the princess and this time, Maddie noticed, even she sounded really worried.

"I'm not sure yet," said Sebastian. "I need to think . . ."

Before he had the chance to say any more, a dark shape suddenly swooped down and the princess gave a little cry of alarm.

"It's all right," said Sebastian. "It's only Zak!"

"Oh, Zak!" cried Maddie as the raven landed beside them on the ledge. "Thank goodness. I was getting so worried about you."

"Well, I'm glad *someone* worries about me," Zak replied.

"I know you can look after yourself," said Sebastian crisply. "Even when you are only skiving."

"Skiving?" squawked Zak. "Skiving? I'll have you know," he spluttered, "that I've been working. I'll have you know," he went on, "that I've sussed out the entire set-up while you lot have been loafing about up here sunning yourselves."

"Is that a fact, Zak?" said Sebastian coolly. "So tell us, what have you found out?"

"Well," Zak leaned back, "for a start, the mountain is hollow."

"We know," said Maddie. "We've just come right through it."

"Oh." Zak looked a bit deflated. Then, plumping out his chest again, he went on. "Well, there's more . . . and you're never going to believe *this* . . ."

178

"Try us." Sebastian threw Maddie a tight little smile.

"You'll never guess who's behind this lot . . ." Zak folded his wings across his chest, clearly proud of what he had learned.

"Try us," said Sebastian again.

"Not in a million years will you guess," said Zak smugly.

"Sebastian said it's the Ice Queen," said the princess impatiently.

"Eh? What?" Zak spluttered, turning his head and gazing at her in astonishment. "How do you know that?"

"We recognized her, Zak," Maddie explained patiently.

"You've seen her?" Zak looked really startled now.

"Yes," Sebastian replied. "She's down there. Look. She's just come out onto the balcony."

Zak turned and looked down to the

plateau where the Sun Goddess could still be seen on the balcony of her temple. "Oh my giddy aunt!" he squawked and promptly put his head under his wing.

"I'd had this strange feeling all along that this whole thing reminded me of something," said Maddie. "And I was right — it is all very much like the Ice Palace . . ."

"Well, this is charming, this is." Zak emerged from beneath his wing. "You send me off to risk life and wing to suss things out and when I get back I find you've got all the answers anyway . . ."

"No, Zak," said Sebastian hastily, "we don't have all the answers, really we don't. And we'd only realized who the Sun Goddess is just a moment before you arrived. But I'm sure you've found out more — haven't you?"

"Might have done." Zak, clearly in a huff now, had turned his back on them.

Maddie inched forward on the ledge and gently smoothed his ruffled feathers. "Please, tell us."

"What?" said Zak, turning his head and squinting haughtily down his long beak.

"Oh, for goodness' sake!" said the princess suddenly. "Stop all this nonsense. That's my brother down there in chains for heaven's sake. What I want to know is how you propose getting him out of this terrible place."

"Zak?" said Sebastian sternly.

"Oh all right, have it your way!" said Zak. "I've been talking to the skylarks," he went on. "They have their nest on the side of the mountain and they seem to know everything."

"Birds generally do," said Sebastian, then when Zak threw him an indignant glance he added hurriedly, "It's a good job too. Don't know how we'd manage

181

without them. Did they tell you what she's doing here?" He jerked his thumb in the direction of the gold-clad woman on the temple balcony who, together with several of the hooded figures on the plateau, now seemed to be bowing down and worshipping the sun.

"Apparently," said Zak, "according to the skylarks, she appeared here one day accompanied by her Devil Bats and announced to the People of the Sun — who, by the way, have lived inside the mountain for donkey's years — that she is their goddess and that they must obey her."

"And they believed her?" asked the princess incredulously.

"It seems so," said Zak. "Don't forget she still has magic. She's been trying out her spells and trying to get them right in a cave on the other side of the mountain. Some of them appeared to go very wrong

and she poured the potions away into the mountain stream . . ."

"And polluted the water . . ." said Sebastian grimly.

"Exactly," said Zak. "She told the People of the Sun, who from what I can make out were a pretty weird lot to start with, that her mission was to build a temple here on the mountain, and to do this they had to recruit many helpers."

"And no doubt those helpers would have to stay after the temple is completed and be her servants for life," said Sebastian. "If they survive the heat and dreadful conditions that is."

"Just like those people in the Ice Palace that she had captured," said Maddie.

"And Frederic is one of those prisoners," cried the princess.

"Well yes, I had worked that one out," Zak replied drily.

"Any ideas on releasing the prisoners,

Zak?" Sebastian turned to the raven.

"Now you come to mention it," said Zak importantly, "I did happen to find something out that may be of help in that direction."

"What's that?" Maddie clasped her hands together.

"The chains securing the prisoners are locked with a single key," said Zak. His voice was so low they all had to lean forward in order to hear what he was saying. "And that key," he went on in the same hushed tone, "is on a ring tied to the belt of that little fat guy down there."

With one wing Zak pointed down to a corner of the plateau where one of the hooded people was sitting on the ground a little apart from the others.

"Apparently at this time of day, after the People of the Sun have finished their bowing and chanting they will go into the temple with the goddess or whoever she

184

is," said Zak. "But our fat friend stays on guard.

"According to my mate the skylark," he continued, "after his pals have disappeared, this little guy relaxes and more often than not, dozes off in the sunshine . . ."

"What are you saying, Zak?" asked Sebastian, and Maddie recognized the edge of excitement in his voice.

"What I'm saying, my son," said Zak, "is that when this happens, I guess it would then be a pretty easy matter for me to fly down and nick the key." He paused. "Which one's the crown prince?" he asked, lifting his sunglasses and squinting down at the figures below.

"That one there." The princess pointed. "The one on the end of the line."

"Oh yes, so it is." Zak peered down. "I'd never have recognized him. He's lost weight. Well, hopefully if I give him the

185

key he will be able to release them all."

"And then what?" demanded the princess. "We still have to get away. I can't see the Sun Goddess or her people just letting us walk out of here ... and then there are those bats ... and her magic spells ..."

"You're forgetting something," said Maddie quietly.

"What's that?" demanded the princess.

"Sebastian also has magic and it will be far stronger than anything the Sun Goddess might have."

"You mean ... the second spell?" asked the princess.

"Spot on," declared Zak with a chuckle. "You've got it in one."

* * *

They waited high on their ledge, unseen by anyone, for what seemed like eternity but which, in actual fact, could not have been very long at all. They saw the Sun

Goddess go back into her temple together with all the hooded figures except the little fat one, who settled himself down on the ground beside the prisoners while they continued with their back-breaking task in the full glare of the afternoon sun.

At last, just as the skylark had predicted, the little fat man's head fell on to his chest and it was obvious he was asleep.

"Right," said Sebastian. "This is what we will do. First, the second spell. Are you ready, Maddie? I'm relying on you. At this precise moment, I have to confess I can't remember one word of it."

"It's all right," said Maddie reassuringly. "I'll start saying it and you join in when you remember."

Sebastian lifted his hand so that the rays of the sun caught the stone in the ring he was wearing. Tentatively, first Maddie, then Sebastian, began reciting

the words of the second spell while Zak and the princess looked on.

"Zimelda of Zimbarwire
Through Orange Molten Fire
Zinggaskium Ze Zingagic
Flare Now and Work Your Magic."

The mountainside was already bathed in sunlight, but as the topaz responded to the spell the sunlight seemed for a moment to grow brighter, and it was then, fairly loudly, but not so loud that anyone on the plateau might hear, Sebastian said, "By the Power of the Topaz may the volcano reactivate after one hour."

The princess gasped, Zak gave a muffled squawk and Maddie covered her mouth with her hand, while the glow on the mountainside deepened to such an extent that even the prisoners paused in their work and looked around in

amazement, until the light faded again and everything returned to normal.

"Whatever do you think you are doing?" demanded the princess.

"I have reactivated the volcano," Sebastian replied calmly.

"You must be crazy," she cried. "We are on the volcano, for heaven's sake! How are we going to get away?"

"Just trust Sebastian," said Maddie.

"Absolutely," said Zak. Cocking his head to one side, he looked up at Sebastian and asked curiously, "On the other hand, just as a matter of interest, old son, how *do* you propose we are to get out of here?"

"This is the plan," said Sebastian, and they all edged closer to him. "I want you, Zak, to fly down and get the key as we arranged. I also want you to tell Frederic that we are here and what is going to happen. Tell him to tell the other

prisoners when he releases them that they have one hour to get away. Then tell him to join us up here. During the panic, when everyone realizes what is happening, we'll make our escape through the crater and back down the outside of the mountain."

"So there you go," said Zak with a shrug as Maddie and the princess stared wide-eyed at Sebastian. "Nothing to it. Easy-peasy."

Chapter Twelve

Escape from Sun Mountain

They watched in mounting apprehension as Zak flew down to the plateau. Maddie felt as if her tummy was tied into knots and when she looked at Sebastian and the princess, the expressions on their faces suggested they were probably feeling the same way.

The raven dipped and swooped, a black shadow in the path of the sun before

he glided in to land beside the first prisoner in the gang. They saw Frederic look up sharply, then guessed that he had recognized Zak, who must have gone on to explain to him what was happening for he looked up towards the ledge at the top of the mountain.

The princess leaned forward eagerly, then as Frederic raised his arm she waved back. The next moment, Zak flapped his wings and flew across the plateau to the little fat man asleep against his boulder.

"Oh dear," whispered Maddie. "I do hope Zak's going to manage to get the key."

"He will," said Sebastian confidently. "Zak is a master of stealth."

"I have to admit," said the princess rather grudgingly, "he's certainly of more use than I thought he'd be."

"He's got it!" breathed Maddie as the raven suddenly flew back to Frederic with the key clearly visible in his beak.

After that it was only a matter of seconds for Frederic to unlock the chains that bound not only himself but all the other prisoners. Before the friends had time even to think what was happening, the prisoners began to disperse in all directions, the little fat man awoke with a start, and Frederic was bounding up the pathway towards them with Zak at his side.

"Lyra!" Frederic cried as he clasped her in a tight embrace.

For once the princess seemed lost for

words and she simply hugged her brother in return. He looked thin and strained, his hair long and unkempt, while his trousers hung from his legs in tatters and his bare feet were bruised and bleeding.

"We have to move," said Sebastian urgently. "Come on, back into the crater."

Together they made their way back through the narrow passage inside the mountain until they were in the vast crater once more.

"We need to get across to the other side," said Sebastian, "then we can escape through the other passage that will take us out on to the far side of the mountain —" He broke off abruptly as there came a sudden commotion further round the crater.

They all froze in their tracks as first a group of prisoners fled around the crater, chased by a bunch of the hooded figures, and then the tall, gold-clad figure of the

Sun Goddess suddenly appeared on the far side.

"Oh no!" gasped Maddie. "There must be another way into the mountain from the temple."

For a long moment the Sun Goddess stood there staring at them with a dark cloud of her Devil Bats flitting and swooping around her, then she gave a shriek of pure rage that echoed round and round the crater, hitting the walls and bouncing back and forth.

"You!" she shrieked as she pointed a quivering, red-taloned finger at Sebastian and Maddie. "You again! How dare you! You tried to destroy me once before! You will not get away with it this time!"

"Oh my giddy aunt!" squawked Zak. "Time we were outta here, old son, wouldn't you say?"

"Absolutely, Zak," said Sebastian. "Absolutely."

They fled around the edge of the crater, away from the crazed Sun Goddess, but just when it seemed they would reach the opening, a group of hooded figures suddenly appeared as if from nowhere on the ledge directly ahead of them.

As Sebastian came to a sudden stop, the friends all careered into him.

"Oh!" gasped Maddie. "Oh, Sebastian what are we going to do?"

For one long, terrible moment they stood there on the ledge of the crater, the People of the Sun on one side barring their exit and the Sun Goddess and her evil Devil Bats on the other.

"Can't you do some magic or something?" screamed the princess as the hooded figures began to edge menacingly towards them.

"I already did," said Sebastian quietly.

And sure enough, at that very moment, when all seemed lost, there came a noise

— a rumbling noise that seemed to come from the very depths of the great mountain freezing everyone in their tracks.

As the hooded figures stopped and listened, Sebastian took advantage of the moment and stepped forward. Drawing himself up and flinging his cloak over his shoulder, he addressed them, his voice ringing out loud and clear and echoing around the vast cavern.

"People of the Sun," he cried. "Listen to me!"

Maddie, who by this time was holding her breath, saw the group of hooded figures hesitate as if uncertain what they should do, then look to the figure of their goddess for instruction.

"You think," Sebastian went on in the same ringing tones, "that this woman is your goddess. You are wrong, quite wrong. She is not. She is an imposter. She was once known as the Ice Queen — she uses

people for her own selfish ends. She will destroy you in time. You must believe me."

"Don't listen to him!" shrieked the woman on the far side of the crater. "Seize them! Don't let them pass!"

As the People of the Sun hesitated in bewilderment at what Sebastian had just revealed, the Devil Bats seemed more agitated than ever and at the woman's frenzied command began flying across the crater towards the friends, screeching as they came.

"Oh no!" screamed the princess, covering her head with her hands. "I hate bats! I hate bats! Stop them, Sebastian. Frederic, do something, please . . ."

And then it happened again, that awsome rumbling sound, only this time it was louder, much louder, so loud that it paralysed everyone around the crater, from the woman in gold to the friends and the hooded figures. Even the bats

seemed frozen for a moment before they turned and flew straight back to their mistress, whimpering with fright.

And this time, along with the rumbling, there came a fierce bubbling noise.

It was one of the hooded figures that first gazed over the ledge into the depths of the crater.

"Aaahhh!" His cry filled the cavern. "It's the volcano . . . it's boiling . . . it's going to erupt!"

Sure enough, far below them Maddie could see an orange, glowing, seething mass that was beginning to boil and bubble.

There was silence for a long moment, then pandemonium broke out as the group of hooded figures turned tail and fled along the ledge away from the friends.

"Come on!" commanded Sebastian. "Now's our chance! Keep close together. Follow me!"

Behind them they could hear the

blood-curdling screams of the so-called Sun Goddess and as Maddie threw a frantic glance over her shoulder just before they plunged into the passage, her last glimpse of the evil woman was of her waving her arms and trying to command the return of the People of the Sun, while her Devil Bats screeched around her head.

Together the friends fled and as they found themselves on the steep path on the outside of Sun Mountain, they realized that people were leaving in droves. In the chaos it was difficult to know exactly who they all were, whether prisoners or People of the Sun, but as they all ran for their lives, the rumbling and boiling noises grew louder and louder.

* * *

In spite of the impending danger Sebastian calmly led his little band down the side of the mountain and back through the pass to Hamish McTavock's abode.

The goat was sitting high on his rock watching them as they approached.

"Would ye mind telling me what in the world is going on?" he demanded. "This pass is getting more like a public highway every day. Just look at that stream of folk making their way over here . . ."

"I think you'll find, Hamish, that very soon you'll have all the peace and quiet you want," said Sebastian.

"What about Sun Mountain?" barked the goat. "Look at it! I've never seen the like."

They all turned to look at the mountain, which until that moment had been so full of secrets and such mysterious goings-on. By this time sparks were flying out of its top and even as they watched it suddenly blew, erupting a great mass of flames high into the air and lighting up the sky for miles around.

"Bless my soul!" cried Zak, hiding his head under his wing.

"Just look at that!" cried Frederic a moment later, as a great sheet of molten lava began to creep down the side of the distant mountain, smothering everything in its path.

"Do you think everyone got away?" asked Maddie anxiously.

"I should say so," snapped Hamish. "They're all heading this way!"

"Everyone had plenty of warning," said Sebastian.

"What about her — the Sun Goddess, or Ice Queen, or whoever she was?" asked Maddie with a shiver.

"She wouldn't want to leave that golden temple," said Frederic. "She probably barricaded herself in there."

"If she has," said Sebastian grimly, "she could well have found herself trapped by the lava."

"Serves her right," snapped the princess. "She shouldn't have people

kidnapped . . . especially crown princes."

"How were you captured?" asked Zak, throwing Frederic a curious glance.

"I was gradually lured into their circle," Frederic explained grimly. "It was all very exciting at the time you know, and extremely pleasant . . ."

"It probably would be, at The Blue Parrot," said Zak with a chuckle.

"They made it sound as if I was going on an adventure," said Frederic. "It wasn't until I was inside the mountain that I realized I was a prisoner of the Sun Goddess and doomed to spend the rest of my life in hard labour." He paused and looked at the friends. "How did you know where to find me?"

"Got a fortnight to spare?" said Zak. "It's rather a long story."

"The Princess Lyra made a wish for you to come home," said Sebastian.

"Did you?" Frederic looked at his sister

in amazement as if it was the last thing he would have expected from her.

The princess nodded but Maddie noticed she looked embarrassed. "We knew you'd been to Zenetzia," she said, "because of the postcard you sent. From there we followed the clues . . . right here to Sun Mountain."

"And now," said Sebastian, "we need to return to Zavania."

"It's a very long way," said Frederic.

"The unicorns will take us," Sebastian replied.

After saying farewell to a still irritable Hamish, the friends made their way down into the foothills, where they found Cornelius and Conrad waiting for them.

The gentle unicorns greeted them with delight and after they had listened to the amazing story the friends had to tell, Cornelius hastened to tell them that his fellow unicorns were growing steadily

stronger as they drank the fresh, pure water from the mountain streams. "And now," he concluded with a toss of his head, "all that remains is for us to take you home."

"Thank you, Cornelius," Sebastian replied. "I will ride with you this time. Conrad will take Frederic, the Crown Prince."

"I'll come with you, Sebastian," said the princess quickly and Maddie's heart sank.

The princess moved towards Cornelius as she spoke but Sebastian held up his hand to stop her. "No, Your Royal Highness," he said. "You ride pillion with your brother. Maddie rides with me."

Sebastian turned to help her mount the unicorn and as he took her hand in his, Maddie felt as if her heart was about to burst.

Chapter Thirteen

The Prize

"And you say the Crown Prince Frederic was a prisoner of this evil woman?" Zenith stared at the friends in horror. It was much, much later, after the unicorns had brought them back to Sebastian's boat, the friends had returned to Zavania, and the prince and princess had gone to the palace to see the queen. "Did she know who he was?" Zenith demanded.

"Oh yes," Sebastian replied. "Frederic says she was well aware who he was and had been from the very start when she had instructed the People of the Sun to entice him into their cult. Apparently it gave her great satisfaction to have him as her prisoner and she took added delight in working him even harder than the others."

"Heaven only knows what else she would have done in terms of ransom demands . . ." Zenith shuddered at the thought of it.

"Well hopefully, this time we really have heard the last of her," said Sebastian.

"With a bit of luck she'll never get out of that temple of hers again," added Zak.

"That was extremely good strategy of yours to reactivate the volcano," said the WishMaster, looking admiringly at Sebastian. "Yes, very good strategy indeed," he added. "Now, tell me," he

went on after a moment, "what did you use the other spell for?"

"To restore the water in the mountain stream," said Sebastian and when Zenith frowned, he went on to explain. "The Sun Goddess had been trying out her magic, which was obviously very dodgy. It seemed every time a potion went wrong, she poured it away into the stream where it polluted the water."

"Disgraceful!" declared Zenith.

"It was poisoning the unicorns," said Maddie.

"And everything else as well by the sounds of it," added Zak.

"Well!" said Zenith at last. "It sounds to me as if you have conducted yourselves in a quite exemplary fashion ..." He paused as Thirza suddenly appeared in the doorway of the turret room. "Yes, Thirza," he asked, "what is it?"

"It's the Crown Prince Frederic and the

Princess Lyra," said Thirza. "They are downstairs. They want to see you, Zenith. They have a message from the queen."

"Ask them to come up," said Zenith. "Then they too can be witness to what I have decided to do."

Maddie glanced at Sebastian and saw that a dull flush had touched his cheeks; she quickly threw a look at Zak, but the raven simply closed one eye in a huge wink. Maddie had a feeling she knew what was coming next, but she couldn't be absolutely certain.

There was no time to wonder any further, however, for at that moment Thirza came back up the stairs to the turret room, huffing and puffing as she accompanied the prince and princess.

"Your Royal Highnesses." Zenith swept a deep bow. "To what do we owe the honour of your presence?"

"Yuck!" muttered Zak under his breath

and when Maddie shot him a warning glance, he added softly, "Well, for goodness' sake! If it wasn't for us they probably wouldn't even be here."

"We bear greetings from Her Majesty the queen," said Frederic solemnly. He looked quite different now, in a velvet tunic and silk hose, from the poor wretch they had rescued from Sun Mountain. "She has asked us to convey her profound thanks and gratitude for the granting of my sister the princess's wish, resulting in my safe return to Zavania." He turned to Sebastian as he spoke.

"It was our pleasure, Your Royal Highness." Sebastian bowed as he replied.

"Our mother, the queen," said the princess, "is so overjoyed about Frederic's safe return . . ."

"You bet she is," muttered Zak softly so that only Maddie could hear, "especially as the king has not yet returned from the

south and therefore need know nothing about any of this."

". . . that she would like to see Sebastian rewarded in some way," the princess went on, throwing Zak a suspicious glance.

"The queen says," Frederic carried on, turning to Sebastian, "that you only have to name your heart's desire and it shall be yours."

"I think," Zenith replied, "that we all know what Sebastian's heart's desire is . . ."

"To gain his Golden Spurs . . . and be a WishMaster . . ." breathed Maddie.

"Which I was about to award him anyway," said Zenith. "He has proved to me beyond doubt that he has the qualities to be a WishMaster even though, at first, he will only be a very junior WishMaster."

He paused and looked round at the others, at Maddie and Zak, both of whom were quite overcome, at Thirza who had

211

tears running down her wrinkled cheeks, at the Crown Prince Frederic, and at the Princess Lyra, who for once was rendered speechless by the occasion. Then he solemnly approached the cabinet on the wall where he kept the spells and rings used to grant wishes.

Maddie found herself holding her breath as Zenith beckoned Sebastian forward, then turned the key in the lock, opened the door and withdrew a glass case. Inside the case and nestling on a bed of black velvet lay a pair of gleaming Golden Spurs.

As Sebastian knelt before the WishMaster and Zenith placed one hand on his head none of the others could hear what was said between them. And then, at last, Sebastian rose to his feet once more and Zenith presented him with the spurs.

"You have great power now, Sebastian," Zenith said in a loud voice. "You have completed your apprenticeship

and are a fully fledged member of the Worshipful Guild of WishMasters. May you always use this power wisely and with the greatest of integrity."

As Sebastian turned, flushed with pleasure, unshed tears gleamed in his eyes and the others broke into spontaneous and happy applause.

"Bravo!" called Zak, flapping his wings as they all crowded around Sebastian to see the spurs. Then, as Thirza began pouring her special strawberry cordial into goblets for a toast, Sebastian turned and looked at Maddie.

"Well done," she whispered, taking his hand and squeezing it tightly.

"I would never have done it without you," he said, his voice husky.

Maddie gulped, unable to speak for the lump in her throat, afraid if she did she might disgrace herself and not only start crying, but even worse, might not be able

to stop for fear that now Sebastian would no longer need her. She was saved from speaking, however, by Zak, who gave a sudden, indignant squawk.

"And what about me?" he demanded. "Don't I get a mention?"

"Of course you do, you crazy raven," said Sebastian, reaching out and ruffling the feathers on the top of Zak's head. "My feelings about you never change. You drive me mad most of the time, but I wouldn't want to go anywhere without you."

This seemed to satisfy Zak, who gave a deep sigh and settled down on his perch for forty winks with his head under his wing.

When the celebrations were finally over the prince said he and the princess had to get back to the castle to report to the queen what had happened.

"And I have to go home too," said Maddie reluctantly. "I have to attend my school prize-giving."

"Maybe you'll have a prize just like Sebastian," said the prince kindly as he took her hand in farewell. "You certainly deserve one. Goodbye Maddie, and thank you again, with all my heart."

As the prince turned away Maddie found herself face to face with the princess. For once, even she seemed subdued and not like the Lyra of old.

"Goodbye . . . Maddie," she said.

"Goodbye . . . Lyra," Maddie replied firmly.

"Thank you," the princess added, "for all your help . . . in granting my wish."

"That's OK," said Maddie gruffly.

"I hope . . ." said the princess.

"Yes . . . ?"

"I hope you'll come back and see us again. You will, won't you?" Suddenly she sounded quite anxious, as if it was somehow important to her that Maddie should do so.

"That's up to Sebastian." Maddie half-turned towards him. "Will I?" she asked.

"Of course," said Sebastian without any hesitation.

"That's all right then," said the princess.

* * *

They left Zavania shortly afterwards and it seemed in no time at all the boat was slipping beneath the willows in the stream at the bottom of Maddie's garden.

"Looks like it's goodbye again, Maddie," said Sebastian as he brought the boat into the bank.

"Actually," said Zak before Maddie could reply, "I was thinking, if you two would like five minutes on your own to say your goodbyes, I could make myself scarce . . ." He flapped his wings.

"What you mean is, there's someone you want to see," said Sebastian dryly, as he stepped ashore.

"I don't know what you mean," spluttered Zak.

"Not a certain little dove?" asked Sebastian.

"Whose name just happens to be Delores?" added Maddie, taking Sebastian's outstretched hand as he helped her ashore.

"Yeah, yeah," muttered Zak. "All right."

"Five minutes, Zak," said Sebastian warningly.

"OK!" the raven snapped before flying off up the garden.

They watched him go, then Maddie gave a little sigh. "I hate this part," she said at last.

"I know," said Sebastian. "So do I. Let's just hope it won't be too long before someone else makes a wish."

"I can't help thinking it will all be different now," said Maddie sadly.

"What do you mean?" asked Sebastian gently, staring down at her.

"Well, now you are a WishMaster and not just an apprentice maybe you won't be needing so much help . . ."

"Maddie, oh, Maddie." Sebastian laughed, then, taking both her hands in his, he said, "You don't think just by becoming a WishMaster it will make my memory any better, do you . . . ?"

"Well . . ."

"I'll still need you to help me remember the spells. I guess I always will."

"Oh . . ."

"But it isn't only that," he went on, growing serious.

"No?" she said, looking up into his face.

"No," he replied. "It's more. So much, much more. It's you, Maddie. It's the way you are. Your kindness, your concern for everyone . . . It's the way you calm everyone down — even Zenith. It's the way you always fight for what you think to be right."

"Oh," she said, quite lost for words.

"I couldn't even think of going on an assignment without you by my side," he said softly, as putting his arms around her he hugged her closely. They stayed like that for a few quiet moments until a crashing in the willows heralded Zak's return and reluctantly they drew apart.

Moments later Maddie stood on the bank waving as the boat slid away, once more carrying Sebastian and Zak the raven back to Zavania, that land of magic where time stood still.

* * *

"Oh there you are," said Maddie's mother as Maddie stepped into the kitchen. "Have you had your lunch? Good, then we'd best get ready for the prize-giving."

The school hall was packed with pupils and parents as the staff made their entrance and filed onto the platform. A series of rather boring speeches followed

during which Maddie daydreamed, slipping quite easily back into the enchanted world that she had just left.

Lucy sat beside her while their mothers sat at the back of the hall with the rest of the parents. Jessica Coatsworth was in the row in front, no doubt preparing herself for the many trips she would be making onto the platform to receive her expected prizes.

"Are you going to the reception afterwards?" whispered Lucy.

"No, I think it's only for prize-winners," Maddie whispered back.

"Well, that's us out," said Lucy. "Oh, here we go," she added as the chairperson of the school governors sat down after her speech and the headmistress took her place in front of the microphone and began reading out the list of prize-winners. She started with the juniors and as she read out each subject and the winner, the pupil went up on to the platform and

received her prize from the chairperson.

"Now it's our lot," hissed Lucy.

"Well, don't hold your breath," said Maddie. "We all know the outcome anyway."

"Sport," said the headmistress, "always plays a great part here at St Benedict's and this year is no exception. There is one girl who has really excelled herself by winning practically every sporting event of the season and I am sure I don't need to tell you who that girl is . . ." She paused as the girls in the row in front of Maddie and Lucy all began nudging each other and grinning. "Jessica," said the headmistress, looking over her glasses with a smile, "come and receive this year's prize for sport."

"What did I tell you?" said Lucy gloomily. "This'll just be the first of many."

They watched as Jessica received her cup, applauding politely along with

everyone else as she returned haughtily to her seat.

The third-year subject prizes came next and to the girls' surprise the Maths prize went, not to Jessica, but to someone else, a girl called Kirsten.

"That shook her," muttered Lucy. "She was definitely expecting that one."

The subject prizes continued with, to everyone's amazement, the prize for speech and drama going to Maddie.

"Oh, well done! Well done," cried Lucy as Maddie, red-faced, came back to her seat with her cup.

"I never expected this," whispered Maddie.

"You deserve it," said Lucy. "Everyone knows you're a star at poetry and drama."

"Am I?" said Maddie in amazement, then, "Oh, Lucy," she cried, "you've got the food technology prize!"

"What!"

"Go on," cried Maddie. "Go and get it!"

Jessica Coatsworth had half turned, a look of disdain on her features, when Maddie had gone up for her prize, but she remained motionless as Lucy stumbled out of her seat and went up to the platform amidst a rousing burst of applause.

The two girls were still recovering from their unexpected triumphs while the headmistress finished the form prizes, completed the special prizes and awards to members of the senior school, and then, with one small cup left on the table, held up her hand for silence.

"Every year," she said, "I award my own special prize to the most outstanding girl of the year. This prize, as you know, usually goes to a girl in the senior school but this year I have decided after much

deliberation to award it to a girl in the third year . . ."

A ripple of excitement ran along the row in front of Maddie and Lucy.

"It goes to a girl who has the constant ability to put the needs of others before her own and who is always cheerful and helpful, sometimes in the face of adversity . . . This year," the headmistress paused and it would have been possible to hear a pin drop in the vast crowded hall, "my special prize goes to . . ."

By this time Jessica Coatsworth, a smug, self-satisfied expression on her face, was half out of her seat.

"Madeleine O'Neill."

There was a moment of stunned silence followed by a gasp which echoed round the hall.

"Maddie!" cried Lucy in delight. "Oh, Maddie, it's you! Go on! Oh go on!"

As Jessica Coatsworth sank back into

her seat in disbelief, Maddie rose slowly to her feet, and amidst a storm of applause walked as if in a dream up to the platform and received the award.

On the way back to her seat she caught a glimpse of her mother's radiant face from her place at the back of the hall.

Maddie slipped into her seat beside Lucy, her heart thumping with joy.

"Oh Maddie," whispered Lucy. "I'm so

pleased for you. I can't think of anyone who deserves it more."

Maddie, still unable to quite believe what had just happened, gazed down at the two cups she had won, the one for poetry and the other for helpfulness, and just for a moment her eyes misted over and through her tears of happiness it was as if she was looking at her own set of Golden Spurs.

Wishes *can* come true . . .

Unicorn Wishes

*In the magical land of Zavania, an unhappy
unicorn has made a wish…*

A baby unicorn has been taken away
from his mother and kept in the royal
castle as the Princess Lyra's pet. Now
he's made a wish to go home, but nobody
knows where that is!

Sebastian and his friends Maddie and
Zak are determined to help. Their quest
takes them deep into the Enchanted
Forest, where a dangerous magic is
lying in wait . . .

Mermaid Wishes

In the magical land of Zavania, a frightened
mermaid has made a wish . . .

Seraphina is desperately ill, almost dying.
Her beautiful golden hair is tangled and
matted, and without her own enchanted
comb she will never recover. She has
wished for it back. But who took it?
Where is it now?

Sebastian, Maddie and Zak must find the
comb, and grant the mermaid's wish.
And they must find it quickly, for
Seraphina is fading fast . . .